PRAISE FC

In Crescent City Moon, Nola Nash conjures a gaslit atmosphere of supernatural dread as thick and heavy as the humid air on a moonlit New Orleans midnight. -- Jeff Zentner, William C. Morris award winning author of The Serpent King and Into the Wild Light

Just in time for Halloween, Crescent City Moon is an imaginative and atmospheric tale steeped in the lore of New Orleans and ringing with the haunted echos of 19th-century past where magic is real, dangerous and rife with unexpected consequences. Part horror, part mystery and part fantasy, Nola Nash's debut is perfect for fans of Anne Rice.-- Steph Post, author of Miraculum

For an opening novel in the Crescent City Series, this story packs a serious punch and sets a high standard indeed for future books. I love anything set in the nineteenth century and particularly the dark coming together of cultures, magic, and superstition of New Orleans. Author Nola Nash has really hit the nail on the head for authentic atmosphere, genre-blending wonders and a truly deep, gritty heart at the center of this thrilling work. Zéolie is a marvelous central figure for the plot, lost yet capable of great power and strength as the plot progresses. The novel comprises intrigue, thrills, action, credible and exciting supernatural lore, and even a little romance story, so overall Crescent City Moon delivers a perfectly balanced package of high-quality entertainment. - Reader's Favorite

CRESCENT CITY MOON

BOOK 1 IN THE CRESCENT CITY SERIES

NOLA NASH

RAMIREZ AND CLARK, LLC

To my family who encourage my bohemian side and only occasionally call me weird. And to the city of New Orleans who inspires name with her magic, mystery, and history.

Crescent City Moon
by
Nola Nash

CHAPTER
ONE

Storm clouds skulked across the sky snarling at the moon and stars as they swallowed them whole. Below, in the descending darkness, the city shuddered.

The Hanged Man looked up at Zéolie, smiling and complacent in his bringing of doom as thunder rumbled over the French Quarter rooftops rattling the panes of glass in the parlor windows. As the sound sent a shiver through her, she could have sworn the Hanged Man winked. Tarot cards had always been a game to her and her friends, deliciously taboo among the society set, but something was decidedly different about this spread. They were just cards on a table, but they carried a weight she'd never felt before. With them was a feeling of finality.

"What does it mean?" Lisette asked leaning over the cards. No matter how many times Zéolie explained the meanings in the pictures, Lisette's sweet simple mind could never hold on to the information. Even though Lisette had no idea what lay in the cards, her laughing amber eyes lost their luster in Zéolie's silence.

Expectation hung thick between the two childhood friends,

broken only by the sound of the raindrops tapping on the house and the hiss of wind outside. "The first one is for your past. The Sun. It represents warmth, love, and vitality."

From the settee in the corner, Lisette's sister Celeste laughed and tucked a curl behind her ear that escaped the bun at the nape of her neck. "Who cares about her past?" Leafing lazily through the daily newspaper, Celeste was oblivious to the gathering sense of doom at the table. "So, is she going to fall hopelessly in love with the man of her dreams?"

Zéolie's graceful fingers gently touched the last card on the table. The future. The Hanged Man. Letting go, sacrifice, and martyrdom. Another shiver raced up her spine. Why should such a silly game make her feel like this? Slowly she answered, "Your future. The Hanged Man."

"He's a funny looking thing," Celeste said tossing the paper aside and sashaying over to look. The man on the card hung from a rope by one leg with his other leg crossed at the ankle over the knee of his straight leg like an upside-down number four. His arms were folded over his chest as if hanging there was merely an acrobat's stunt. Confident, yet unnatural in his position. Defiantly pleasant.

"Zéolie, what does it mean?" Lisette asked quietly, ignoring the teasing of her older sister.

"It means you'll meet a mysterious young man," Zéolie answered. The lie settled in her chest, cold and heavy.

"He should be easy enough to spot hanging upside down like that!" Celeste laughed again, sending a ripple through the tension.

This time, Zéolie forced a laugh, too, as she gathered the cards quickly into the deck and shuffled them. Even as the tarot cards slid through her hands, they felt different. They seemed to tug at her palms wanting to be seen. She needed a distraction. "Look at us sitting around playing fortune-teller when there's a party to plan!"

Lisette seemed happy to be carried along with the change in subject. It was as though she sensed a shadow pass over her friend over the last spread that made her as anxious as Zéolie to get away from the cards and on to something less mysterious. "It'll be the party of the season! Julien Cheval's daughter doesn't turn twenty-one every day!"

"It'd be strange if she did." Celeste stretched out on the settee. Her long legs draped over the arm of the chair in a most unladylike way. Feminine propriety was a concept completely lost on the girl.

"Celeste, honestly," Lisette scolded.

"What? Who's here to care how I sit?" her sister demanded with a dismissive wave of her hand.

Lisette shook her head full of wayward dark curls and settled into an armchair near the desk where Zéolie was rifling through the drawers looking for something.

"Ah, ha!" Zéolie exclaimed and pulled out a crumpled paper. Aging wood of the desk chair creaked in objection at even her delicate weight as she sat. "I had a list of all the party preparations, but of course I can't find it. I'll have to start over." She pressed on the edges of the page with the palm of her hand trying to insist that they lay flat. It was a useless effort. The paper was as disheveled as her thoughts.

Celeste tugged her hair out of the bun and let her auburn waves fall over her shoulders as she shook them loose. "For the third time, if I recall." Celeste was right. It seemed that lately anything to do with Zéolie's twenty-first birthday party went missing. Zéolie knew it was just carelessness from all the excitement, but it was beginning to get irritating. "Let me keep the list this time so it won't go running off," Celeste said lazily winding a strand of hair around her finger.

Zéolie laughed. "I don't think so. You'd have cases of champagne, a full orchestra, and acrobats added to the list!"

"Well, of course. How else will dear Lisette ever meet her hanging man?"

There was that chill again as thunder rolled over the roof punctuating the dread she felt. Zéolie dismissed it and focused her efforts on recreating the list. For the third time. Her father would have final say on anything she decided on, but he wasn't one to deny her anything. Truthfully, she didn't ask for much, so there was little occasion for him to reign in his daughter's extravagancies. Zéolie was happy to have the help, even if Celeste spent more time teasing than actually helping.

"Mama said she would be happy to help make arrangements for you, since..." Lisette trailed off and lowered her eyes. A rosy blush colored her cheeks.

"It's alright, Lisette." Zéolie gave her a warm smile and a wink. "And, thank her for me." For some reason, it always seemed to bother Lisette that Zéolie had no mother to take care of parties and other things that mothers would normally do. For Zéolie, it was normal since she had never known her own mother. Her father told stories of the woman he had loved and lost, but the only motherly attention she ever had was from Delia, her nanny, who was more family than servant. As long as Zéolie could remember, the Haitian served the family as nurse, nanny, and housekeeper. Even though she was getting on in years, Delia was still very much in charge of the household affairs. "Delia's handling arrangements for food, but I'd love your mother's opinions on the flowers."

Lisette beamed and her bright eyes sparkled. Zéolie knew that would make Lisette feel better and give their mother something to busy herself with. The widow Marchon was a loving mother, but also a formidable woman. If there was anything that made Madame Marchon happy, it was giving an opinion on something. With so much to do, Zéolie was happy to delegate the task of flowers to her.

"And I'll help you choose a gown. I saw one in Scanlan's window that would be ravishing!" The twinkle in Celeste's eye was all too familiar.

Zéolie laughed and tossed a stray black lock over her shoulder. "And by 'ravishing' you mean 'scandalous.' I saw that neckline. Papa would definitely object to that one!"

Celeste waved off the protest and rolled her eyes. "Nonsense. You'll be twenty-one and he won't have anything to say about it."

Thunder rumbled lazily in the distance as the storm wore itself out. The rest of the evening passed with Celeste planning to scandalize the neighborhood and Lisette prattling on about flowers while trying to talk sense into her sister. It seemed the only one who still remembered the Hanged Man was Zéolie. As much as she wanted to let the card drift into the recesses of her mind, it refused to stay there. For the rest of the night, the Hanged Man dangled at the edges of her thoughts.

THE HOUSE in the middle of Dauphine Street swarmed with activity the day before Zéolie's birthday celebration. Cart traffic coming and going with deliveries rivaled even the riverfront warehouses. Madame Marchon was in her glory directing the florists where to place each and every bouquet of hibiscus and hydrangea blossoms. Garlands of greenery and white roses draped the staircase that swept up the front hall and festooned the intricate iron gallery railings on the front of the house. The back courtyard burst into bloom thanks to burgundy hibiscus topiaries and bright yellow lilies in large painted clay pots. Small tables draped in white linens had been brought in and placed around the fountain. Candles and small vases of single hibiscus blooms in the center of the tables made the courtyard look more like an outdoor cafe. Kerosene lamps on iron stands were strategically placed where they would light the darker corners in an effort by Madame Marchon to keep wayward young couples from lingering in the shadows. Zéolie was quite certain that Celeste would somehow manage to circumvent even her mother's best deterrents.

By the evening, furniture in the parlor had been moved to clear room for dancing, tables outside were ready, and all seemed to be in place. The night would be mercifully free from rain and the morning sun would be enough to steam the dew from the table linens and encourage the perfume of the flowers to fill the house and courtyard before guests arrived. Everything was perfect.

"You have to admit, that woman has a remarkable way with florists," Monsieur Cheval said taking in the courtyard transformation.

Zéolie laughed. "If only she had as much command over Celeste."

Monsieur Cheval shook his head, the silvery gray at his temples shining in the lamplight. "That girl. The man who marries her'll have his hands full." Zéolie's father took his daughter's graceful hands in his and gave them a gentle squeeze. "I still can't believe you're turning twenty-one already. I remember when you were chasing stray cats out of the courtyard, bringing me frogs from the fountain, and asking me to kiss a scraped knee." His eyes grew misty as he spoke but smiled down at her. "That little girl is all grown up now."

Zéolie smiled up at her father and rested her head on his strong chest. He was warm and smelled faintly of a fine tobacco and oiled leather. Smells the little girl in her remembered from nights curled up in his lap listening to stories of her mother. "I'll always need you, Papa," she said squeezing him a little tighter. "I always have."

Her father stroked her glossy black hair falling in loose waves around her shoulders. "That's a sweet thought, cherie, but we both know it's not true. Now," he said putting his finger under her chin, "it's time you get to bed. We can't have you greeting your guests and yawning."

Zéolie took one last look around the parlor. "I don't know how I'll be able to sleep tonight!" Her father laughed, kissed her on the cheek, and sent her up to bed.

～

FOR WHAT SEEMED LIKE HOURS, Zéolie watched the moonlight dance among the folds of the netting around her bed and listened to the night sounds of the city. Wagons lumbering down uneven cobbles, shouts from the riverfront echoing off the buildings, and the faint tinkling of a ship's bell. The French Quarter bustled with activity well after dark and then settled into a quiet hum of locusts. Occasionally, the wind would blow through the close-set houses in a lonely low whistle. As she lay in bed, her mind went over and over the preparations for the party, certain she'd forgotten something. Zéolie checked off things on a mental list as she gazed through the misty netting and out the window into to the night.

Just as she began to drift, she woke with a start. In the flawed rippled glass of the windowpanes, she saw a woman with wild black hair and stormy eyes. Angry, but laughing. Terror seized Zéolie's throat that threatened to shriek. She blinked hard and the image was gone. Nothing remained in its place. Not a shadow of what she was certain she'd seen. Her heart racing, she took several deep breaths and gathered her wits about her.

"I've got to get some sleep," muttered Zéolie hoping the vision was just exhaustion playing with her mind. She pulled the sheet closer around her. The night was warm, but she couldn't shake the chill from her fright. Soon, a restless sleep finally came.

Zéolie saw her father come and sit on the edge of her bed. He lovingly brushed a strand of hair from her forehead and kissed her cheek. She grinned up at him, but he didn't return the smile. Sadness settled in his eyes that she didn't understand.

"I've failed you, Zéolie," her father said slowly. "All these years of protecting you and now I've failed you."

"Papa, you've never failed me!" she insisted. "You've done more than any daughter could ask for."

He shook his head sadly. "No, mon cherie, I couldn't stop her." Over and over he said it shaking his head as tears rolled gently from weary eyes. "I couldn't stop her...I couldn't...I couldn't..." As he sat looking down at her, Julien Cheval's face began to change. Softness vanished from his eyes and his mouth became a thin rigid line. His strong jaw set firmly as his teeth clenched. There was a hardness

Zéolie had never seen in his expression. In his eyes, she was certain she saw fear. "She's coming, Zéolie. *She is coming!*" Cracks began to streak across his face like fissures in an earthquake. His eyes sank deep into the sockets and vanished leaving gaping black holes. Zéolie watched in horror as his lips peeled back revealing a ghastly grin. She scrambled backwards away from the garishness before her, opening her mouth to a silent scream. Her legs curled under her and she clutched at the bedpost, digging her fingernails into the polished wood. Julien's skin began to fall away like cracked flaking plaster, raining crimson onto the bedlinens. Zéolie shrank away in fear and revulsion as her father reached out for her with a hand gnarled and shriveled like a long-dead corpse. Her heart pounding relentlessly in her ears, she finally found her voice and shrieked in terror.

Zéolie woke up screaming and drenched in sweat. It was a dream. A horrible nightmare. As she gasped for air, she realized hers wasn't the only scream in the house. "*Delia!*" Zéolie cried and raced out of her bedroom. Bare feet flew down the hallway following the sounds of Delia's sobbing and screams to Julien's bedroom. Zéolie threw open the door and stood frozen on the threshold. There, behind the netting, was the same horrible vision that terrified her in her sleep. Her father's body was contorted into an unearthly position. Limbs and joints pointed in directions they were never meant to go. His leathery flesh was pulled taut over his bones, his lips curled back in a horrible snarl, eyes sunken in their sockets.

There was a thud on the planked floor as Delia fainted. Zéolie gripped the doorframe to keep from fainting herself. "What the hell happened?" she cursed.

A burst of deafening laughter filled the room. Zéolie's hands flew to her ears, but it didn't help. Instantly, she realized the sound was in her own head. "'*She's coming, Zéolie!*'" mocked a woman's voice. "Fool! The great Julien Cheval thought he could stop this?" More laughter shook Zéolie to her core. She dug her fingers into her scalp in pain and fell to her knees in a crumpled heap. Wind began to swirl through the room; its intensity matching the maniacal laughter. The walls shuddered, and floorboards creaked. Windows thrashed in their frames. As suddenly as it started, the wind and laughter stopped, leaving a vacuum of silence.

For a moment, Zéolie didn't dare to raise her head from the floor. It had to be a nightmare. Her father was sleeping in his room and she was having a terrible dream. Slowly, she opened her eyes. No, this was no dream. This was a nightmare, but she wasn't asleep.

CHAPTER

TWO

The spray of white flowers that adorned the front entrance for Zéolie's birthday celebration was replaced by a black wreath signaling a death in the family. Madame Marchon roused the florist from his sleep before dawn and waited in the shop overseeing every detail of the deceptively simple creation. The groggy florist offered to come hang the wreath out of respect for the Cheval family, but Madame Marchon sent the poor man back to bed and saw to the task herself. The fewer people there were to ask probing questions, the better. Especially since there were few answers to give.

News and secrets were hard to keep in the close proximity of the French Quarter. Narrow alleys and courtyards did little to separate neighbors and offered only a façade of privacy. Screams from the previous night roused neighbors on either side of the Cheval residence and brought the entire block to the aid of the two women. Police were fetched, but the only person who truly mattered to Zéolie was Father Antoine. Madame Marchon tried to convince Zéolie to take a sedative and sleep, but she insisted on seeing the priest. He finally arrived with the gray light of dawn.

"Precious child," the old priest cried as he came into the front parlor. Madame Marchon curtseyed and left them to talk. Zéolie knew the poor woman couldn't bear to hear the horrifying details of the night again, and there was much to be seen to in the house.

"Father, I'm so glad to see you," Zéolie said wearily. Dark shadows were draped beneath her beautiful dark eyes and her face was drawn and pale.

Father Antoine kissed her outstretched hand and gave it a squeeze, then sat next to her in the parlor darkened by curtains pulled shut against the harshness of the sun. "Cherie, you look as though you'd seen a ghost."

"I'd rather that than what I've seen," Zéolie replied. Shock and grief were doing battle in her mind and heart. She didn't know whether to scream or cry, and so she did neither.

"The stories from the neighborhood are horrifying, child. What can I do to help?" the priest offered gently.

Zéolie sighed. "I'm not sure. I'm not even sure about what I've seen and heard anymore. It makes no sense- no logical sense, anyway. It can't be real." Zéolie's voice trailed off and she gazed into empty space before her. Father Antoine didn't press the young woman for more information given her fragile emotional condition. Instead, he rang the small brass desk bell hopeful there was someone nearby to hear it.

Soon, one of Madame Marchon's servant boys appeared in the doorway. He shuffled his feet and refused to look up at the priest or Zéolie. "Father, did ya ring, suh?" he asked quietly, wringing his dark hands nervously.

Father Antoine smiled warmly at him, but the nervous boy didn't look up to see it. "I did. Would you kindly ask Madame Marchon to come sit with Mademoiselle Cheval?" Father Antoine placed his hand on the boy's curly head. The child peeked up at the priest, gave a tiny bow, and scampered off to find his mistress.

∾

FATHER ANTOINE SAT QUIETLY by Zéolie while he waited for Madame Marchon's return but did not pressure her to speak. In a way, he was grateful for the time to consider the facts that seemed more surreal and nightmarish than truth. The officer who came to fetch him explained that Zéolie and Delia were found unconscious on the floor of Julien's bedroom in the wee hours of the morning by a neighbor who heard the cries in the night. After seeing the grotesque corpse, the neighbor ran out of the house screaming for help but refused to go back inside. It wasn't until the police arrived that someone managed to get Zéolie and Delia revived. Zéolie refused to go to bed, but Delia was led to her room as if she were in a trance.

As the priest sat lost in thought, Madame Marchon appeared in the doorway to the parlor. She silently exchanged places with Father Antoine on the settee and took charge of watching over Zéolie. Since he had been unable to gain any insight from the traumatized young woman, he made his way upstairs to Monsieur Cheval's bedroom.

OFFICERS RESPONDING to the cries for help had soon raced back out of the house to vomit and collect themselves. Even with all the bizarre and violent crimes in the history of New Orleans, the sight that met them in the Cheval house still shook them to their core. Gas lamps were turned low to ease the shock of the scene, but all that accomplished was to create eerie dancing shadows that intensified the supernatural sight. Preferring to leave the investigation of the body to Father Antoine, the police focused their efforts on the exterior of the house looking for answers they would never find.

Silent prayers followed the cleric up the stairs. With each step, the leaden weight of grief made his feet harder to lift. By the time he stood on the threshold, Father Antoine's body was as weary as his heart. Even the priest drew back and cursed at the sight of Julien Cheval's corpse. Lingering a moment in the doorway, he mouthed a prayer. Taking a slow breath to steel himself for the gruesome task at hand, he took a cautious step closer. Father Antoine performed last rites for hundreds, watching the light of life flicker and fade leaving only an empty shell where a soul had been. So many times, he'd been called to bless a body found cold and dead, never flinching from the task. This, this was different. This was unnatural.

Father Antoine crossed himself several times and held tight to the crucifix on the end of his rosary as he approached the dead man's bedside. Standing several feet away, the priest tried not to think of the man who sat in Mass only days before. He tried not to picture the strong, elegant gentleman bowing his silver-streaked head in prayer next to his equally striking daughter. The image of that man in contrast to the horror before him was almost more than the cleric could bear. Instead, he tried to distance himself from the memory of the man he knew and focus on the mystery before him.

Behind the netting and in the flickering shadows of the gaslights, Father Antoine could see little in the way of blood-staining on the bed sheets. There were spattered drops on the pillow, but nothing else. It wasn't just blood that was missing, either. He realized that all the fluids that should hace been in the body were unaccounted for.

Father Antoine took a step closer to the bed and noticed something else - or rather, the absence of something. There was no sickly-sweet stench of death in the room. Instead, there was a faint scent of an earthy herb he could not quite place. In all the gruesomeness, there was a fragrance that was almost fresh and clean. "Sage," he murmured to himself as it dawned on him what the herb was.

"Very good, Father!" a woman's voice said. Father Antoine spun around to find the owner. No one. Laughter seemed to fill the room from nowhere and everywhere at once. The room shook as the priest stood his ground, his old heart thundering against his ribs. He knew that voice and it terrified him, but he couldn't let her see that, wherever she was. She couldn't know there was a cold sweat standing out in beads from every pore as her laugh rang through the room.

Defiantly, he called out, "You can't cleanse what you've done here with incense. You can't take murder away with sage."

More laughter, a sick girlish giggle. "Father, why should I try to cover what has been done? He brought this on himself, and he can rot here. I just don't care for the stench of death. The smell of sage is much more pleasant, don't you think?" the disembodied voice asked sweetly.

"*You* did this!" Father Antoine snarled at the voice even as his knees threatened to buckle under him. "Julien is not to blame for this, you demon woman!"

Her sweetness vanished, and the room echoed with her thunderous rage. "Julien thought he could keep her from me and he paid for his crime. Time's up, dear Father. The child is a child no longer. She is free, and she is *mine*!"

The glass globes of the hurricane lamps shattered into glittering shards, and the flames leapt into the air illuminating the mutilated corpse in the bed. The flickering of the fire and shimmer of heat over the body gave the illusion of movement. Father Antoine drew back from the bed but refused to back down from the voice. "*No!*" he screamed. "You may have managed to pull yourself from the squalor of your own hell, but you can't take her by force and you know it! Never forget that. Zéolie will *not* bend her free will to your rage. She will *never* belong to you!"

"And how do you plan to stop me? Julien tried, and it was his undoing." The voice chuckled as though pleased with her own handiwork.

Father Antoine fought to still the shaking of his aged hands that belied his fear and rage. "I don't need to stop you, witch. She'll do that herself once I tell her the truth. For twenty-one years, I've held my tongue, but no more!"

"Now, now, we can't have *that*, can we?" Her words dripped like rancid syrup in the air around the priest. "You'll pay for your treachery, old man!" roared the woman's voice. "All of it! Take a good look, Father!" The flames leapt higher still in a blinding light. Father Antoine shielded his eyes from the heat and the sight before him. "This is how you will be remembered, my dear cleric!" Shrieks and laughter reverberated off the walls as the priest sank to the ground.

Over the din, he screamed in defiance, "Our Father, who art in Heaven, hallowed be Thy name!"

"Save your breath, Father," the voice spat. "Give your lord my regards!" Wind whipped around the room and flames swirled high and wild. Then, as suddenly as it started, the wind stopped, and the flames were extinguished. In the blackness, the priest lay motionless on the floor by Julien Cheval's bed; his hand, still clutching his crucifix, went cold.

CHAPTER
THREE

"Madame Marchon?" The young officer in the parlor doorway spoke so softly she almost didn't hear him.

"Yes," she replied. "Something's wrong, isn't it?" The look on his face spoke volumes.

Lowering his gaze, he answered, "Father Antoine has been found...on the floor..."

Zéolie broke free of the trance of grief that had gripped her. "On the floor?" she asked weakly.

The officer looked at her with strain showing around his dark blue eyes. Walking over to where she stood, and barely above a whisper, he said, "Yes, mademoiselle. He's.... dead."

Zéolie swayed where she sat and fainted into his arms. Madame Marchon gave a cry of shock, but steadied herself on the arm of the settee, then sank down onto it. "Your name, officer?" Madame Marchon asked with her face in her hands.

"Saucier, madame. Louis Saucier, and I'm at your service," the young officer replied as he carefully laid Zéolie on a chaise.

"Officer Saucier, please, get her out of this house. She's not safe here." Madame Marchon pleaded.

The young officer glanced over his shoulder at the older woman. Even with the house swarming with police, a man of God had dropped dead amid a sea of broken glass under a soot-stained ceiling. No one heard anything or saw anything. Somehow, the unthinkable happened completely unnoticed. Zéolie was not safe here. No one was. "Of course, but where? And do you think she'll go willingly?"

"She'll listen to me." Madame Marchon stood and gripped the arm of the settee seeming to need the support to gain control of her emotions. White fingers dug into the tapestry of the upholstery. Head bowed, she pushed a strand of her graying auburn hair away from her face and tucked it behind her ear. Taking a deep breath, she once more took control of the situation. "It doesn't really matter if she goes willingly or not. She can't stay here."

Fanning Zéolie wasn't helping to revive her. Instinctively, Officer Saucier pulled a vial of smelling salts from a pocket as he talked. "I can escort her to your house, madame, if you think she'd prefer to be with your daughters. I'm told they're very close."

Madame Marchon smiled, but it quickly died on her lips. "Yes, like sisters, but she'll want answers that won't be found with us. And she needs prayers in large numbers. The convent. Take her to the Ursulines." Officer Saucier raised an eyebrow at the mention of the nuns given the fate of the priest but said nothing. Madame Marchon lifted her head and met his eyes. "I've been close to this family for years and there are things I know that few have been privileged to. Julien was Zéolie's whole world. It won't be easy for her to swallow that he may not be what she imagined him to be. He was indeed a great man, but, if the rumors are right, he was also a great keeper of secrets. They may just be hearsay, but there may be enough truth in them to guide her. The mother superior would know for certain."

Zéolie started to come to. Long black eyelashes draped on pale cheeks began to flutter as consciousness found her again.

Officer Saucier shook his head and a sandy curl fell onto his forehead. He absently pushed it back into place. "My apologies, madame, but I'm not following."

Madame Marchon rose and walked to the chaise. "Call a carriage and let your superior know what I've asked. I'd like you to come with us if he'll allow that. Once we reach the Ursulines, we'll discuss rumors."

Officer Saucier nodded and, with one last glance at Zéolie, he bowed and went to carry out the orders.

Zéolie watched him go through a fog of confusion. "What's going on? Nuns? Rumors?" Her head pounded mercilessly. Deep in the shadows of her mind was a low laugh that would not relent, distracting her already confused thoughts.

Madame Marchon placed a cool gentle hand on the white cheek of the girl she loved like her own daughters. "You aren't safe here, cherie, so I'm going to take you to the only place I can think of that you might be. The Ursulines will take you in and give you a place to stay. And, my precious girl," she said kneeling beside Zéolie and taking her hands, "you desperately need the prayers."

Numbness settled over her making the surroundings feel sluggish and thick. Thoughts formed slowly as she tried to process what was being said to her. Prayers. Would prayers silence the voice in her head? Would they take the image of her father from her mind? Zéolie nodded at Madame Marchon but had a sickening feeling nowhere was going to be truly safe.

CLATTERING wheels outside came to a halt as the carriage Madame Marchon requested arrived to take the women and Officer Saucier to the Ursuline convent in the Ninth Ward. Helping them up, the captain assured the women he would do everything humanly possible to get to the bottom of what happened. "Humanly possible," Madame Marchon said over her shoulder, "may not be enough." His face whitened as her words drove home, but he said nothing as he closed the carriage door. Instead, he whistled to the driver and stood watching them pull away.

Cold loneliness of grief seeped into Zéolie's veins as she shivered even in the warm closeness of the carriage. Wrapped in a blanket, she gazed out the window as the French Quarter faded into the Faubourg Marigny, then finally to the Ninth Ward. Buildings huddling close together stood sentry as her carriage passed. Baleful eyes of tall windows watched her go by. Colors so vibrant in the sunlight seemed to wash pale in her pain. Zéolie's mind raced with thoughts of her tortured father, the woman's shrieking voice, and the kind priest she'd known her whole life. There were so many thoughts battling for her attention, but she couldn't summon the energy to speak about any of them.

Officer Saucier sat opposite her looking out of the window, but with a more focused attentiveness. Not knowing what he was actually looking for, his eyes traveled over the galleries and shadows for anything out of the ordinary. It was New Orleans. Ordinary wasn't easy to define. Thoughts churned as he sorted through what he'd seen at the Cheval house. He turned them over in his mind, searching for meaning where he couldn't find sense. It didn't matter where he took the women. He knew they were far from safe. If someone could reach Zéolie and her father inside their own house and leave no clues of a point of entry, where else could that evil find her? And the priest murdered under their noses. Louis was certain the danger facing them was otherworldly even though he struggled justifying that with his rational mind. What he could do against a supernatural force he didn't know, but he was damned if he wasn't going to try.

Soon, the red roof and expansive galleries of the new Ursuline convent appeared in front of them. Behind the length of the main building and additions, the Mississippi River churned frantically toward the sea, oblivious to the peace of the sweeping oaks and sleepy gardens. Sanctuary.

Gravel crunched under the wheels of the carriage as it rocked to a halt. A servant had been sent ahead on horseback to announce the arrival of the women and officer to the nuns who waited outside to greet the arriving carriage. Heavy black robes of the sisters matched the somberness of the three guests. Officer Saucier bowed to the mother superior as he stepped from the carriage and handed down Zéolie and Madame Marchon.

"Thank you, Mother, for welcoming us," said Madame Marchon as the older nun took her hand and gave it a gentle pat. Zéolie was gathered up by two young novices who took her inside where a bath was being drawn for her.

"Of course," Mother Micheaux replied warmly. "Such tragedy." The old nun tisked and shook her head sadly. "I'm glad you brought her to us. We can offer little in physical protection, but our prayers are mighty. It will do Zéolie some good to wash the day away. While we wait, I think you could all use something to eat. In times like these, we spend so much time taking care of others that we forgeet ourselves." Leading her guests to the courtyard, the mother superior

DEFTLY STEERED the conversation to mundane pleasantries giving her guests some relief from the emotioinal nightmare of their last twenty-four hours.

"Zéolie should be ready to join us soon," Mother Micheaux said after a while. "Shall we wait for her in the parlor?" Once the dishes were cleared and a plate set aside for Zéolie, Mother Micheaux led them back through the convent to the guest parlor. The furnishings were simple but tasteful. Several chairs for visitors, small side tables with lamps, and little else. Guests of the nuns would be comfortable in the room, but mindful of where they were. With no sign of the opulence found in the French Quarter homes, there was an elegance in its simplicity. Other than the chapel, this was the most furnished room in the building. Areas kept for the sole use of the nuns were even simpler still, containing not much more than a bed and small table. Little else was needed in the largely self-sustained compound.

Madame Marchon smoothed her skirt as she sat in the chair offered to her by the mother superior. Officer Saucier looked as awkwardly out of place as he must have felt in the convent parlor, nervously shifting his weight from one foot to the other and his hands shoved deep in his pockets. Mother Micheaux offered him a seat as well. "Young man, we're glad to have your company," she said warmly. "We don't have many gentlemen visit us, but an officer is always welcome. I only wish the circumstances were more pleasant."

"Thank you, Mother," he replied. Taking a deep breath and sitting down, Officer Saucier was only mildly successful in trying to appear more relaxed than he obviously was.

"Now, let's get to the real reason you're here. Madame Marchon, I'm guessing choosing us as sanctuary was more than a need for prayer and a secluded space," Mother Micheaux said as she sat and settled her robes. Aging hands absently adjusted the large wooden rosary hanging from the belt at her waist before folding serenely in her lap. The mother superior had an air of elegance that mingled with the warmth of understanding. Officer Saucier knew she had been high-born and the only one in her family to have taken the veil. A path that had clearly been the right one. Mother Micheaux's leadership was renowned in the diocese, as was her compassion for the people. Often seen in service where needed, the mother superior seemed to take the term 'cloistered' with a large grain of salt.

Madame Marchon answered, "As always, Mother, you're very perceptive. I was hoping you could offer some clarity to the situation, or, at the very least, answers that may give Zéolie some direction."

"I'll do what I can to help, of course. The events of the last night are indeed tragic, especially the death of Father Antoine." The aging nun's voice faltered as she thought of her friend and fought to keep her composure. Crossing herself, she drifted into a reflective stillness, seeming to forget she had guests in the room.

Officer Saucier broke the silence after a few moments. "Mother," he began gently, "the police have no clues to go on. Anything you can offer would be greatly appreciated."

Mother Micheaux gazed for a moment at the young officer before she spoke. Strength rested in her expression, but something else flickered behind her eyes. "Louis, that's because there aren't any clues to be found. At least not where the police are looking."

Zéolie appeared at the doorway. "Then, where should they be looking?"

The three in the parlor looked up at the young woman, who was now wearing the borrowed dress of a young novice, her black hair in damp loose waves over her shoulders. Even in the simple clothes, her beauty and grace remained intact.

"W-we've searched the house and grounds," Officer Saucier stammered, clearly taken with the vision in the doorway.

"Have you discovered anything?" Zéolie asked taking the chair offered by Mother Micheaux. Washing the events of the night away did her some good. At least enough to let her focus on getting some answers.

"No," he answered dropping his eyes to the floor wishing he had something to say that would sound less hollow than the truth. "Nothing. It was as if no one entered the house."

"Probably because no one had," replied Mother Micheaux.

Zéolie's brow knit in thought. "I'm sorry, Mother. After every-thing that's happened, I'm not thinking clearly. I don't follow what you're trying to say. What do you mean no one entered the house? How could this have happened otherwise?"

Mother Micheaux walked over to Zéolie and took her hand. Wrinkles creased the thin white hands of the nun, but her fortitude flowed through them into Zéolie's. "You've been through so much, and it's getting late. Maybe this would be a conversation best left until morning."

Dark eyes glittered with rising tears as the young beauty tried to force a smile for the mother superior. "With all due respect, Mother, there won't be any sleep for me if I don't get some answers. My father's death, the sight of him like that—" Zéolie's voice cracked as she broke down. Sobs wracked her frame and pain and sorrow poured from her soul in a stream of heartbroken tears.

Officer Saucier pulled a handkerchief from his pocket and knelt by her side, gently offering it to her. Blinded by tears, she took it from him and buried her face in it. Giving the young woman time with her pain, Mother Micheaux sent one of the novices to fetch a glass of brandy to soothe Zéolie 's frazzled nerves. Another novice began to light the lamps around the parlor to ward off the darkness brought on by the setting sun. Madame Marchon rested a comforting hand on Zéolie's shoulder for a moment but said nothing. There were no words that could staunch the flow of emotions. No words that could turn back time and give her back her world.

After a few moments, Zéolie's sobbing quieted and her breathing began to return to normal. "Thank you," she said as she accepted the glass of brandy he held out to her. She sipped it quietly for a moment, letting it flow through her. Sinking into the warmth of the brandy, she began to relax from the strain. "I'm so sorry." Her words were barely a whisper, and her stinging swollen eyes focused on the glass in her hand.

"Child, there's nothing to apologize for," Mother Micheaux said putting her arm around Zéolie's shoulders to steady her. Even though it was small and frail, there was strength in it of one used to bearing the spiritual weight of others in it. "If this is too much to talk about now, it can wait."

"No," Zéolie insisted. "Please. I need to do this."

"Alright," replied Mother Micheaux taking her seat once again. "Zéolie, tell me, was there anything unusual before you discovered your father's death?"

Zéolie nodded and closed her eyes to concentrate on her memory. Images of the night swirled in front of her eyelids, a kaleidoscope of terrors slowly coming into focus. "Yes," she began slowly, "as I was drifting off, I thought I saw a face in the window, which makes no sense with my bedroom on the second floor." As she spoke, her hands began to tremble. Afraid she'd spill what was left in her glass, she set it on the side table beside her. In her lap, Zéolie's hands twisted as she continued, "The party preparations left me exhausted, but excited, so I was having trouble sleeping. I know I imagined it, but I can't shake that image. It seemed so...real."

"Can you describe what you saw for Mother Micheaux?" Officer Saucier asked more comfortable in his role as detective.

"It was a woman with wild black hair. Her eyes......they looked angry, yet almost seemed to laugh. I can't explain it."

"Then what?" Mother Micheaux prodded gently.

"I slept but had a terrifying dream that wasn't a dream." Zéolie told the mother superior about the dream in detail, talking through the tears that streamed down her pale face. "I didn't know what he meant by 'She's coming, Zéolie,' but when I heard the voice in his room, I knew he meant her. But who is she?"

"I can't tell you with any certainty who he meant, but I have a very good idea," Mother Micheaux said shaking her head. "However, there's someone here who may be able to help you find the answers you need. Sister Angelie."

Officer Saucier, who had been silent for some time, said, "I don't understand. How can she help?"

"There are some things we don't understand or speak of," Mother Micheaux began. "The Church tells us that these things don't exist or are the work of the devil. Sister Angelie was brought to us as a child because of certain...gifts she possesses. Her parents were devout Catholics and hoped time with us would cure her of what they called 'possession.' Truthfully, they were afraid of her. She could see things and knew things she shouldn't. For years, she's called this convent her home. Angelie's taken the veil and is a loving and faithful sister, but her gifts remain. She's been given a very special task. Sister Angelie tends the grave of Camille Cloutier."

Zéolie and Officer Saucier looked confused, but Madame Marchon simply stared back at the older nun. "So, that much is true."

Mother Micheaux nodded. "Yes. When the convent moved, many

of the graves of the departed sisters were exhumed and moved to the grounds here. Camille's was not."

"Because of the legend?" Madame Marchon asked settling back into her chair. Her hands gripped the soft arms as though she feared what she would hear next.

"Wait!" Zéolie interjected, her head throbbing as she tried to follow the tangled threads of the conversation. Trembling fingers pressed into her temples trying to stem the pain and silence the haunting laugh that lurked in the shadows of her mind. "It feels like you're talking in riddles. What legend? Who are you talking about?"

"I'm sorry, Zéolie," Mother Micheaux apologized. "Let me back up. A generation ago, a ship arrived in New Orleans and on board was Camille Cloutier, who'd been forced out of France on suspicion of witchcraft. Camille brought with her a fortune and her young daughter, Solène, but was taken ill on the passage over. Once in port, the captain had to figure out what to do with the deathly ill noble-woman. Rains had delayed the completion of the house she ordered to be renovated for her arrival, and the hospitals were full of yellow fever patients. With no other choice and a ship to turn around, the captain arranged for his passenger and child to be brought to the old convent in the French Quarter.

"I was a young novice then, but I remember the day she arrived. The captain ordered the sailors who brought them to keep quiet about the rumors of her exile, but word had already spread through the Quarter by those tongue-waggers working on her house. There was a witch on her deathbed in the convent."

"But what does a dying witch have to do with any of this, and where does Sister Angelie come in?" Officer Saucier asked. He paced as he listened to the story, watching his own feet as he walked. Far from ignoring the mother superior, his mind was working over every detail, turning them over in his mind to see every possible angle.

"Solène was my mother's name..." Zéolie whispered as the story began to sink in. Her mother was the child of a witch. Blood ran cold in her veins as the laugh rose from the recesses of her mind.

Mother Micheaux nodded. "And Camille was your grandmother. She died within a fortnight of her arrival. Even as she succumbed to the illness, she was kind to those of us who cared for her. We began to doubt the rumors we'd heard. The witch-hunts of Europe and Salem had spawned legends of women who used their powers to torment rivals and ensnare men, but this woman was different. She was kind and grateful. The sickness had robbed Camille of her strength, but not her striking features. Raven black hair that shone like silk and those eyes..." Mother Micheaux paused and looked at Zéolie and smiled. "You favor her a great deal, cherie.

"Camille worried constantly about the health of her little girl," the nun continued as she stood and walked to the window. Absently, she fidgeted with the edge of the curtain as she spoke. "Solène had run of the convent and played and laughed with all of the sisters who tried to keep the seriousness of her mother's illness from worrying the poor child. Her dark eyes would sparkle as she giggled with the novices who chased her down the halls. She was strong and vibrant. Even with death looming, there was such life here with her. No one knew what had brought on the fading health of her mother, but whatever it was, it hadn't touched the child."

"Why didn't my father tell me any of this?" Zéolie asked no one in particular.

"I'm sure he had his reasons," Mother Micheaux answered with the wisdom of someone who knew more than she let on. Something that was not lost on Officer Saucier, whose eyes narrowed slightly.

"Camille died quietly one night surrounded by the sisters with their voices raised in song," the nun continued. "I watched from the doorway as Mother Superior performed last rites even though Camille never asked her to. Solène had been brought in for a final blessing from her mother and stayed with Camille clutching her hand until the end. The poor child collapsed in tears as her mother took her dying breath. When Camille died, it was if the light left the room leaving us in darkness amid dozens of flickering candles." Mother Micheaux's gaze was lost in her reverie. Quietly, she continued, "Solène sat in my lap on the floor and I rocked her. She used the edge of my veil to dry her little tears. Solène, what did we do wrong, sweet angel child?" she asked the heavens.

No one spoke as the mother superior stood lost in her own memories. Her eyes grew misty and a single tear trickled down her cheek. Curiosity and confusion tugged at Zéolie to ask what Mother Micheaux meant, but she thought better of pressing her about it just yet.

A young nun came to the door and tapped on it quietly. "Mother?" she asked.

Mother Micheaux tore herself from her thoughts. "Yes, sister?"

"It's time for Vespers. One of the elder sisters has offered to lead them if you'd like."

Mother Micheaux nodded. "Please, thank her for me. I'll see to our visitors and join the service shortly."

Madame Marchon rose from her seat. "It's late and I should get home to the girls. Officer Saucier, will you be riding back with me?"

The young officer nodded. "I'll see you safely home, then I'll come back to the Ninth Ward station. The officers here need to know what's going on in case..." he trailed off not wanting to upset Zéolie. "I'll stay the night at the station if you need me, Mother. Several officers will stand guard outside tonight, if you permit it."

Mother Micheaux nodded. "A wise suggestion, Louis. Thank you."

Madame Marchon hugged Zéolie and gave her a kiss on her cheek. "Try to get some rest, cherie. Things'll seem clearer in the morning. And there are arrangements to consider as well." Zéolie nodded and wiped the tear that slipped down her cheek.

Officer Saucier took Zéolie's hand and kissed it. "Zéolie, I'm so sorry for your loss. We're going to do everything we can to find out who did this. If you need me..."

"Thank you, officer," Zéolie said blushing under his gaze.

"Louis."

"Louis," Zéolie repeated. Louis smiled, released her hand, then followed Madame Marchon to the door.

Watching him go, Zéolie could still feel the warmth of his hand around hers and a tingle where his lips grazed the back of her hand. A flutter darted up her arm and danced through her heart as the voice in Zéolie's head chuckled softly.

CHAPTER
FOUR

In the silence of the night away from the center of the French Quarter, the river lapped at its banks in soft slaps. Night birds sang low melancholy songs that floated on the cooling damp air. Darkness enveloped a starless inky sky. Under the frame of the rough-hewn window on a tiny bedside table, a low lamp flickered warding off the blackness on the other side of the wavy glass. A small puddle of light washed over the table's edge onto the worn wooden planks of the floor. Warmth played along the stark plaster with tiny cracks like threads snaking across the walls that seemed to move with the dance of the flame.

As exhausted as she was, sleep did not come easily to Zéolie. Events from the night before and the story of her mother's past from Mother Micheaux haunted her. Every thought of her father brought a new flood of tears. Sorrow settled over her in the night like a blanket of lead. Heavy and unyielding. Closing her eyes only brought images she never wanted to see again to her mind. A madwoman in the window. Her father's sneering mangled corpse. Then there was the low laugh haunting her mind since her father's death that came and went all night. By the time the sun crept above the horizon and the morning bells chimed, she'd been sitting awake for hours.

Sister Angelie met Zéolie in the parlor after breakfast was cleared. Dressed in the traditional black robes and wimple, she was as non-descript as her vocation called her to be, but beneath the habit was a truly unique nun. "Maybe some fresh air would do you good. The garden's actually quite nice this early in the morning," Sister Angelie suggested.

"Sounds wonderful. Thank you, Sister."

"Please, call me Angelie. 'Sister' sounds too formal." The young nun smiled warmly at Zéolie and put her instantly at ease. Angelie led the way to a garden behind the convent, nodding in greeting to the officers standing guard at a respectable distance.

Dew-jeweled flowers and leaves sparkled in the soft early morning light. Shadows of the sweeping oak trees provided cool pockets of air in the gathering humidity. Soon, the sun would steam the droplets away and the flowers would droop in the heat. But, for the moment, the garden was truly a sanctuary.

"I love to walk here in the morning," Angelie said softly running her hands along thick waxy leaves. Dew rolled down and fell in sparkling drops onto the brick path. "Nature has so much to teach us, but we're often too busy to listen."

"What does it tell you?" Zéolie asked. Angelie was kind and welcoming, but as Zéolie watched her move through the garden, it was easy to see that the young nun existed somewhere between the worlds of the living and the dead. Her demeanor was both grounded and ethereal.

"Nature speaks its own language. I suppose what I get is more like a feeling." Angelie smiled half-heartedly. "But the garden isn't really why you're here," the nun said turning to face her.

Zéolie shook her head and sighed. "Truthfully, I'm not completely sure why I'm here. It seems like everyone around me is talking in riddles and I can't guess the answers."

Angelie nodded thoughtfully, then turned slowly away and sat on the branch of a live oak that reached into the ground and swept back up again. She braced her feet on the upsweep of the branch and settled onto the down sweep. "Sometimes, when I need to clear my head, I come here. When I was a little girl, there was a tree like this behind our house. There's something comforting in this old tree." The oak was kind enough to have done this more than once, so Zéolie was able to follow the sister's lead on a nearby limb. Sitting in the tree with Angelie reminded her of lazy summers with Lisette and Celeste. Those carefree childhood days seemed so distant somehow. For a while, the two young women sat in silence each lost in their own thoughts until Zéolie finally broke the silence to ask a question that had been swirling through her reverie. "Angelie, Mother Micheaux seemed to think you could give me some anwers she couldn't. Do you think she's right? Can you help me find out why all of this is happening?"

"I'll be happy to share anything I can with you, but I might be as confusing as the others," Angelie said after a moment. "You see, I only know part of the story myself."

"At this point, I'll take what I can get," Zéolie said.

"Then, I'll tell you whatever I can." Angelie hopped off the branch and brushed dust off her skirt. "Horses. Your clothes are here."

Zéolie hadn't heard anything, but as soon as the words left Angelie's mouth, from a distance came the soft clatter of hooves and the creaking of carriage wheels. Moments later, Madame Marchon's coach rumbled up to the door and her men unloaded a trunk of Zéolie's clothes. Clearly, she was not going home anytime soon.

Once she was dressed in her own clothes, Zéolie began to feel a bit more like herself. Madame Marchon sent a note along with her things telling her not to worry about arrangements for the funeral as she would take care of them. Relief mixed with the guilt and grief that washed over her. As much as Zéolie thought she should plan her father's service, she was grateful to have someone else in charge of decisions like that. At the moment, there were more pressing questions to answer than what sprays of flowers should be in the church.

LOUIS SAUCIER HADN'T SLEPT much that night, either. Questions with no answers swirled through his mind as he lay in the unfamiliar cot in the Ninth Ward station. For much of the night, he tried to ratio-nalize what he'd seen in the Cheval house in the Quarter and what he'd heard in the convent parlor. As an officer, it wasn't in his nature to believe in superstitions and ghost stories, but he was beginning to doubt his practical logic in this case. Nothing at the house on Dauphine made any sense, and the answers he hoped the Ursulines could provide only raised more questions.

And then there was Zéolie Cheval. Tragic, beautiful and mysteri-ous. There was something about her Louis couldn't put his finger on. Something that captivated his imagination. He thought back to when he had to tell her about Father Antoine's death. She'd collapsed in his arms. For a moment, the world had vanished.

"Get hold of yourself," Louis told the half-shaved man in the speckled mirror. "She's a victim in an investigation. That's all." He wondered how many times he would have to lie to himself before he believed that.

Louis arrived at the convent just after lunch to find the officers standing guard had changed for the day shift. They nodded at him from the shaded corners they found to escape the heat of the day and he nodded in answer a bit half-heartedly. What were they going to do against the force facing them? The men knew enough to be on the look-out for anything suspicious, but not much else. The officers in the Quarter knew what happened, but these hadn't been part of that. Louis and his superiors agreed that the fewer rumors to deal with, the better. Confidentiality was not something the department could count on.

Mother Micheaux was sitting at her desk when Louis was shown into her study. "Come in, Louis. Please have a seat," she said waving him to a worn wooden chair.

"Thank you, Mother." Louis sat across the modest desk and noticed how much more formidable the aging nun appeared in this official setting. He stifled a yawn behind his hand. "Excuse me. I didn't get much sleep."

"I can imagine. Zéolie says she slept, but I doubt that. I have to admit it was a restless night for me, too. So many memories and mysteries at once," she said folding aging white hands on top of the desk.

"That's actually what I came to talk to you about," Louis began. Even though it seemed wrong to pry into the memories of the mother superior, he had a job to do and she was the only one with any answers. "When you spoke of Zéolie's mother, you seemed to think that you'd failed her in some way. Can I ask what you meant by that?"

The nun sighed, sat back in her chair, and closed her eyes as if trying to picture the memory. After a moment, she said, "When Camille died, there was no one to look after Solène. We tried contacting family in France, but mother and child had been disgraced and no one would claim her."

"No one? But she was just a child."

Mother Micheaux shook her head. "And she was such a precious little thing. It broke our hearts. By that time, we'd become quite attached to her. Rumors about her mother made it difficult to find a family to take her in, much less adopt her. So, she stayed with us. It was hoped that her seclusion would help to dispel the rumors and she'd get an education - both academic and religious."

"How long did Solène stay here?" Louis asked.

"Until she married Julien. She was eighteen and he was twenty." Mother Micheaux paused and sighed. "Solène loved him at first sight and who could blame her? He was sophisticated and handsome. Not to mention very well off."

Louis wrinkled his brow. "His family must've been thrilled with his choice," he said with more sarcasm than he intended.

"There are occasions when even women of God must stretch the truth. By this time, our hopes of stifling the story of Solène's mother had worked. The story of her noble French lineage was the one we focused on. It was said that her parents sent her to us for an education and had tragically died of disease while she was away."

"Just enough truth to be believable."

"Exactly," Mother Micheaux answered with a twinkle in her eye.

Louis ran his hand through his hair as he thought for a moment. "How did you handle the lack of inheritance?"

Mother Micheaux laughed, creases deepening at the corners of her bright eyes. "Camille handled that one for us."

"How—" Louis stammered, the furrow in his brow getting more pronounced as his confusion grew.

"We assumed that, since Camille had been run out of France as a witch, any property she had would have been seized leaving nothing for her daughter to inherit. However, Camille somehow managed to secure everything before she left Paris, including the house she bought here. Before she died, Camille had a will made that left everything she owned in France and in New Orleans to Solène. It wasn't until the death of our mother superior a few months before Solène's engagement that the secret was discovered among Mother's papers. The mother superior was the only one with any reservations about the marriage. She was very firm about the convent being the best place for Solène. Once the mother superior died, it seemed Fate worked everything out for Solène, with both an inheritance and no one to object to the marriage, making her a suitable match for Julien."

Louis leaned back in his chair. "Curious timing."

Mother Micheaux paused. "Hmm. I hadn't thought of that. I guess it was. Knowing what I know now, it does seem rather fortunate timing." Mother Micheaux frowned and thought for a moment.

"You don't think Solène was in some way responsible for the papers turning up at that time, do you?"

"Now that I think about it, I wouldn't put that past her. I also wouldn't put it past her that she had something to do with the death of the mother superior."

"How did she die?"

"It was an illness that came on suddenly. No one knew what it was. She just began to fade in strength and vitality. There were no symptoms of cholera or yellow fever. Just a malaise that seemed to take her down..." She paused, then her eyes locked with Louis'. "Just like Camille." She began to shake her head as tears welled up in her eyes. Drained of color, her face went deathly pale under her black veil. "How could we have been so blind? How did we not see the connection?" White hands shook as the mother superior wiped a tear that stole down her cheek.

Louis offered his handkerchief to the nun who dabbed at her eyes and began to collect herself. He waited until she recovered her composure before asking, "There was no suspicion about the mother superior's death at the time?"

"None. She was older and had taken ill. None of us suspected anything. I suppose we should have when the papers turned up, but we loved Solène and thought it was a wonderful discovery of a key to her future happiness. But it doesn't make any sense. How would she benefit from the mother superior's death unless the nun was hiding the inheritance? And there would be no reason for her to hide them except that she was trying to keep Solène in the convent."

Louis nodded. "Maybe the mother superior feared she inherited her mother's abilities and thought the convent walls could contain what she'd become. And maybe Solène didn't want any part of a convent prison. Not that it could really hold her if that was the case."

"If only we'd thought about it then," she said shaking her head. "Now, there's no way to prove it." Creases and wrinkles deepened with Mother Micheaux's guilt.

"Even if there was, there's nothing to be done now," Louis replied in an attempt to take some of the distress off the mother superior. The formidable nun that sat behind the desk when he came in was fading as she talked of Solène and the mother superior. Dwelling on that part of the story wasn't going to give him any answers and was only causing the nun grief. "Tell me about Solène's marriage to Julien Cheval," he said steering the conversation to something less emotional. "Was it a happy one?"

"For a few years. She did love him very much and he loved her." Mother Micheaux's expression lightened some, but the shadow of painful memories refused to let go. "Julien gave her everything she could've asked for and more. Solène loved to host balls and intimate gatherings. Their house was always full of guests and she was such a charming hostess.

"And then things began to change," she said, shadow settling heavily on her features. "Julien travelled extensively and would send her tokens from every place he went. These used to bring her so much joy, but after a while they didn't anymore. Solène began to grow sullen and withdrawn. We thought she may be lonesome and invited her to stay with us while he was away. She never replied to the message, so I went to see her." Mother Micheaux paused and shook her head. "She'd changed drastically. Her skin had become almost ashen and there were dark shadows under her eyes."

"Was she ill?" Louis asked.

"That was my first thought. Solène angrily refused my offer to send for a doctor and ordered me out of the house. She'd never spoken to me like that before."

"What did you do?"

Mother Micheaux shrugged. "What could I do? I left, but I spoke to her doctor anyway. He had no idea she was in that condition and was concerned for the child."

"Zéolie?" he asked. The mother superior nodded. "Could the pregnancy have been responsible for the change in her, then?"

"It could've," Mother Micheaux replied. "However, even ill, most expectant mothers are happy to share that news. It seemed Solène was angry at the world at a time she should've been celebrating. Something wasn't right about that."

"Did you mention it to her?"

"No, I thought if she wanted us to know, she would've told us." The mother superior stood and paced the small office as she sifted through the past. "Maybe she was afraid something would happen to the baby and wanted to keep it to herself for a while. And there was plenty that could've gone wrong with so much pestilence running rampant through the Quarter. Yellow fever was raging at that time, and fear of it was running high in the city. People were evacuating, and bodies were piling up in the morgue. Fear for the safety of her child would've been enough to cause the extreme change in her. It would've accounted for the seclusion, too."

"True," Louis said. "Did Julien know?"

Mother Micheaux shook her head and tapped her fingertips on the polished wood of the desk as she thought. As she explained, she rose and paced the small office floor. "Julien was away on business for two months. When he returned home, he was worried about the drastic changes in his wife and came to see me. She hadn't told him anything about the baby. Out of concern for the health of mother and child, I told him what I knew. Of course, Julien was thrilled, but hurt that Solène kept it from him.

"As time went on and the birth grew nearer, Solène seemed to come back to herself a bit more, although she remained pale and withdrawn until the end." She stopped her pacing and sat on the corner of the desk, pushing a stack of papers to one side.

Louis fidgeted with his shirt cuff in thought as he continued to pull information out of the nun. The more he questioned her, the worse he felt prying into her memories like she was some common suspect in a criminal investigation. "I was told Solène died not long after she had Zéolie. That had to be a difficult time for Julien."

Mother Micheaux nodded. "Extremely. A little while after the birth, even in her weakness, Solène was fiercely protective of her child. She would allow no one to take the baby from her and spent hours whispering in Zéolie's tiny ears. Julien thought it was sweet, but the servants would tell you she was cursing the child. One dared to tell him so and was swiftly punished by being sent to the plantation to work in the fields."

"Damning punishment for a house servant. I can't imagine any others had anything to say after that," Louis said shaking his head.

"No. They feared for their own skins, so they said nothing. More had to know something about Solène and her drastic changes, but they were too afraid to speak out. However, that didn't prevent them from talking out of their master's earshot."

Louis let out a short sarcastic laugh. Most of his best leads had come from the mouths of servants who had a chip on their shoulder and were happy to give just enough information to get their masters in trouble without putting their necks on the line for spilling it. "So, slave stories bred the rumors Madame Marchon spoke of?"

"For the most part, yes," replied Mother Micheaux. "There's some truth in them to be sure, but where that line is between fact and fiction, I can't tell you."

"Which is why you suggested Sister Angelie."

"Correct again, Louis."

"Solène's funeral must've been hard on all of you after raising her for so many years," Louis said sadly.

Mother Micheaux's eyes grew misty as she thought for a moment. "I'm not sure any of us were ever able to truly let go of her," she replied softly.

It was an odd response, but Louis didn't want to bring more pain to the aging nun by pressing the subject any further. He had a lot of history concerning the Cheval family, but nothing to go on for the current investigation. Bowing to Mother Micheaux, he thanked her and took his leave. Louis desperately wanted to see Zéolie but wasn't sure if it was because he had a professional reason with the story he just heard, or because he hadn't been able to get the vision of her standing in the doorway in the novice's borrowed dress out of his mind. Even in simple garb, she was stunning.

CHAPTER

FIVE

L ow laughing in her mind had turned into a singsong, but Zéolie couldn't understand the words. It swirled in with her own thoughts, dancing through them, giving her a dull headache. She was doing her best to ignore it, and the voice seemed satisfied with remaining in the background. For the moment, anyway.

Zéolie hurried down the long corridor to the front parlor to meet Sister Angelie and the carriage driver who would be taking them to the French Quarter site of the old Ursuline Convent. Rounding the corner, she ran smack into Louis, tripping over the hem of her skirt. Once again, Louis found himself with Zéolie in his arms as he broke her fall.

"Oh! I'm so sorry!" Zéolie said blushing and trying to free her foot from the tangle of skirt and petticoat. The more she struggled and wobbled on one leg, the more tangled she got in the layers. Even as she untangled herself, part of her wanted to stay wrapped in the strength of his arms.

Louis held her elbow to steady her until she managed to extricate her foot. "It's alright. Girls don't usually fall over themselves to get to me, so it's a nice change," Louis said with a laugh and a twinkle in his eyes.

Zéolie giggled and straightened her skirts trying not to lose herself in the warm woodsy smell of his aftershave that clung to her hair. "What a picture that must've made in the middle of the convent!" Even in her embarrassment, it felt good to laugh.

Louis grinned and blushed. He hadn't thought about where he was with his arms full of French socialite. "Where are you going in such a hurry?" he asked as they started down the hallway.

"Back to the Quarter with Angelie."

Louis' smile faded, and a chill ran through him. "Zéolie, I don't think that's a good idea. At least not until we have a better idea of what we're dealing with."

"I'm not going back to the house," she said dismissing his concern. "We're going to see Camille."

"Look, I can understand you wanting to see your grandmother's grave, but I don't think the Quarter is safe for you right now." Or anywhere else, he thought.

Zéolie stopped and turned on her heel to face him. "Louis, whoever she is, she could have killed me when she killed Papa and Father Antoine. She didn't. There must be a reason for that. The laugh in her mind seemed oddly amused at her words then settled back into a deep chuckle. "I have to find out what's happening, and Camille is the best place to start."

Damn. She had a point. "How do you know that Camille hasn't sent whoever this is?" he asked in one more attempt to keep her from going.

Zéolie shook her head. "Angelie wouldn't take me to her if she feared Camille. I can't explain why, but it feels like the right thing to do. I've got no other answers and only more questions, so I have to start somewhere." She paused and looked up at the concern on his face. "Come with us," she said gently laying a hand on his arm.

Louis thought for a moment. As much as he didn't want her to, he knew Zéolie would go with or without him. He sighed as his better judgement evaporated. "Alright, but on one condition—the instant I suspect you aren't safe, we leave."

Zéolie beamed up at him, her black eyes dancing. "I can live with that."

Sister Angelie was waiting for Zéolie in the foyer. The novice seemed completely unfazed by Louis' presence as if she had expected him to join the outing. "I'm glad you could join us."

"Louis, this is Sister Angelie," Zéolie said.

"Please, just call me Angelie."

"Angelie it is, then," Louis replied with a bow to the sister. "Thank you for your help. We're in desperate need of some answers and it seems all we find are more questions."

"I'll do what I can, but I don't know how much help I can be."

"At this point, we'll take whatever we can get," Zéolie said.

Midday sunshine washed over them before ducking behind a large white cloud sending beams in all directions from the silvery edge as the trio made their way out to the waiting carriage. The slightest breeze off the river stirred tiny clouds of dust on the drive in front of the convent. After handing the women up, Louis informed the officers standing guard of the plan to go into the Quarter to track down some information on a lead. He was intentionally vague since it would have seemed ludicrous to be going to see a long-dead grandmother for information. Even Louis wasn't sure there was anything to be gained, other than protecting Zéolie and Angelie, but he went along anyway—his logical mind be damned.

THE RIDE into the French Quarter from the Ninth Ward wasn't long, but the road was congested with cart traffic and pedestrians. Wagons loaded with crates tied down with ropes from the ware-house district outside the French Market lumbered awkwardly along the uneven streets. Women walked side by side congesting the banquettes telling secrets and rumors behind lace-gloved hands.

Men followed behind, equally as frustrated with the ambling females as much as their own manners that prevented them from going around. Ahead, a crash and clatter followed by clinking glass brought the carriage to a momentary halt as a wagon ahead hauling a precarious pile of furniture overturned spilling half its load on one side of the street. Men jumped off the front seats of several carts and carriages to help pull the load to one side to keep traffic moving. The delay as the carriage tiptoed though the crowd was a good opportunity for Louis to fill Zéolie in on his chat with Mother Micheaux. Angelie half-listened as she gazed out of the window at the passing houses and people. Every now and again, she would shudder as if she caught a chill, but the day was warm and humid. Zéolie knew Angelie must have seen or felt something they couldn't but didn't want to ask what it was. Besides, there was too much to take in from Louis' story.

Zéolie's head swam from the heat, the rocking of the carriage, and the deluge of information as they pulled up to the old convent that now belonged to the bishops. Hard edges and gray stucco rose up in front of them with none of the peaceful warmth of the new convent in the Ninth Ward. Above the chapel that sat at a right angle from the living quarters was a tiny cross gleaming white against a turquoise sky. In front of the imposing structure was an expanse of open lawn. Warm rays of dappled sun splashed across the façade that was trying so hard to be cold and distant. Priests and bishops walked in quiet conversation, while a few others strode with purpose in or out of the large wooden doors. Angelie was well known on the property and no one seemed surprised to see her there, but curious glances were directed at her companions as they walked to the far edge of the yard.

"Our guide doesn't say much, does she?" Louis whispered as he and Zéolie trailed behind Angelie across the lawn.

Zéolie shook her head. "No, but then, everyone seems to be talking in riddles lately, so maybe fewer words are best." Louis nodded, and they continued to walk in silence.

Moments later, they arrived at the far corner of the property framed by a gray stone wall that stood between the sin of the city and the convent's holy residents. Angelie stopped and waited silently on her companions to catch up with her, hands folded demurely at her waist. As Zéolie drew nearer, she began to feel strange. Hair on the back of her neck stood on end and a tingle of electricity raced down her spine. There was a closeness around her, even in the wide-open space of the former convent's garden. It was as if someone were walking right behind her, step for step, breath for breath. The singsong in her head began to change back to the low, mocking laugh. Angelie locked eyes with Zéolie. Had she heard it, too?

"Are we almost there?" Louis asked, wiping sweat from his forehead with a handkerchief.

Angelie smiled. "This is it," she answered her hand outstretched above the grass beside her. There was no headstone; no indication at all that there was anything different from any other piece of grass.

Louis looked at the ground and squinted. Surely, he misunderstood. "But there's nothing here. Mother Micheaux said you tended Camille's grave. It's just grass. What's there to tend?" Louis asked, his confusion growing. Maybe it was the stifling heat of the afternoon or the stench of the waste in the Quarter, but his head was swimming and he was having a hard time understanding how this could be the right place.

"What'd you expect?" Angelie asked.

With an exasperated shrug, he replied, "I'm not sure. It's just that it's the grave of a witch-" A hard look from Zéolie cut off Louis' confused rambling. "Sorry, Zéolie. *Suspected* witch. I guess I expected a stone at least."

"I admit, I expected there to be something tangible, too," Zéolie added looking at the non-descript patch of grass.

Angelie looked at Zéolie. "But you know we're in the right place, don't you?"

Prickling cold ran through Zéolie's body followed by gentle

warmth. It was as if there was a tug-of-war in her mind. Her eyes closed as the low laugh grew louder.

Louis watched as Zéolie began to sway gently. Not sure if she was going to faint from the heat, he reached out a hand to steady her.

"Stop!" Angelie hissed at him. "Don't touch her. Let her feel it. She's got to feel it for herself."

"Feel what?" Louis whispered.

"Shh!"

Zéolie's hands flew to her ears as the laugh grew louder. "She can't help you, cherie," the voice mocked. "She's dead. There's nothing here! Foolish child. To think she'd be there for you!" The voice roared with laughter, then resumed its singsong. Zéolie staggered forward a step and the voice grew quieter. Another step. Softer still. The closer she got to Camille's grave, the more the voice faded into the distance. Finally, Zéolie sank to her knees in a vacuum of silence.

Angelie and Louis watched as her face softened from the clenched pain a moment earlier. Her body relaxed, and her hands fell away from her ears. Peace settled over the chaos of her mind. Eyes still closed, she smiled.

"She knows she's here," Angelie whispered.

"Who?" Louis asked, not taking his gaze off Zéolie.

"Camille knows her granddaughter has come. She's calmed the storm in her mind," Angelie said smiling contently.

Louis was beginning to understand how Zéolie felt about the riddles. "I—I don't understand," he said turning to the nun for answers he knew she wasn't likely to give.

"She's right," Zéolie answered, opening her eyes. Her placid expression darkened as she explained. "The laughter and the song stopped. That maniac's been laughing at me and singing a ridiculous song since last night."

"What'd she tell you?" Angelie asked.

"You can't hear her? But I thought maybe—" Zéolie broke off.

The novice shrugged and shook her head. "It doesn't work like that. I knew you were hearing her, but I can't hear it. I could see it in your face earlier."

Zéolie stared down at the ground in front of her. Tiny blades of green swayed in the sultry breeze. A warm pressure settled on her shoulders, but it didn't frighten her. It felt comforting and strong. Taking a deep breath, she explained, "The voice I heard when I found Papa. It never really left me. All night long, she's been quietly laughing. Then, she started singing, childish and nonsensical. I can't tell what the song is. The words aren't clear, but it seems familiar somehow." Zéolie paused, certain Louis thought she was crazy.

"Why didn't you tell me?" Louis asked.

"Would you have believed me if I did?" Zéolie countered.

Louis shrugged and ran his hand through his curls. "I find myself believing more and more things these days."

Angelie took Zéolie's hand and squeezed it. "But she said something to you, didn't she?" the little nun prodded.

As much as Zéolie didn't want to think about the voice for fear of bringing it back, she focused on what she'd heard. "Yes. The laughing became deafening again. She was mocking me for coming. She said I was a fool for thinking Camille would be here for me."

"Do you think she was right?" Angelie asked sitting cross-legged on the grass next to Zéolie.

"No, she's here." Zéolie's eyes closed again as she let herself feel the presence of her grandmother. Pressure on her shoulders, quietness of her mind, and a sense of tranquility that enveloped her. In the peace, there was power, not the raging of the madwoman. Strength that didn't need to be forceful to be felt. A cool breeze stirred the grass and pushed tendrils of her dark hair across her face as she sat entranced in the moment with her grandmother.

Louis watched as Zéolie's face relaxed into a contented smile. She lifted her face up to meet the breeze and he knew she was safe here. Finally, there was a place where she could find some escape from the tragedy that surrounded her. Louis looked down at Zéolie's beautifully serene face and lied to himself once again. *She's a victim in an investigation and nothing more.* Angelie smiled at him. She knew.

Zéolie finally broke the silence that hung in the humidity of the Old Convent garden. "I can feel her," she whispered. "I don't know how, but I know she's here. That's why you brought me here, isn't it? To see if I can connect with her, too. Angelie, can you talk to her?"

The nun shook her head and absently twisted a blade of grass around her finger as she spoke. "Not always. I was hoping you could. I don't hear her speaking to me like I hear you or like you hear the voice in your head. It's hard to explain. It's more like I know without actually hearing the words. That's one of the reasons I said I may be more riddles than help."

Louis sat on the ground next to Zéolie. A flutter danced through his chest that he blamed on the heat and stress. "Angelie, if you can't hear Camille, how is it that Zéolie can hear the other voice in her head so clearly?"

Angelie shrugged. "I don't know. Honestly, I haven't known anyone else with gifts like mine until now. The sisters are supportive, but they don't really encourage my talents. They certainly haven't made a point of helping me understand them."

"But Mother Micheaux doesn't seem to have a problem with what you can do," Louis said.

"True, but she's afraid if certain people on the outside discovered the gifts it would be dangerous for me."

"But she told *us*," Zéolie said.

Angelie nodded. "Only because of the family connection to Camille. She never would've mentioned it otherwise."

The three sat in silence, each lost in their own thoughts. The breeze continued to cool the air around them and the sun nestled between the French Quarter rooftops. Long shadows stretched lazily across the lawn. Sounds of horses and carriages clattering by, the occasional shout, and bells from the cathedral were distant to them even though they were just over the stone wall. The background sounds lulled them all into a sense of peace and calm.

Louis picked at a blade of grass and Angelie let a ladybug walk up the long black sleeve of her habit. Zéolie sat with her hands flat on the ground in front of her that was the unmarked grave of Camille Cloutier. Thoughts wandered back to her house on Dauphine. The horrors of death were pushed from her mind as memories of happier times with her father washed over her.

For a moment, it was as if she was home walking through the house. She saw herself climbing the sweeping front stairs to her room and laying across her bed like she did when she was small. At the foot of her bed, in a tiny rocking chair, was the rag doll she had as long as she could remember. Julien said her mother made it for her before she was born, and it was the only connection that remained of Solène.

"You need to go home," Angelie said breaking the silence of Zéolie's reverie.

Zéolie sighed. "You're right. It's getting late."

"Yes," answered Angelie, "but I meant you need to go back to your house. There are things you need to know there."

"Great, more riddles," said Louis as he got to his feet and brushed dirt and grass from his wrinkled trousers. "You aren't going back there." Louis paused as Zéolie's eyebrows went up. "I- I'm sorry. I didn't mean for that to come out as an order," he said, blushing. "I just can't let you go back to that house where so much has happened. It's not safe."

Zéolie's expression softened as she looked up at him. "She didn't hurt me, remember? She could have, but she didn't. I don't think hurting me is what she wants."

Louis looked into her pleading eyes and the smile that was developing the nasty habit of disarming him. Against his better professional judgement, he relented. "Only if you have a full police escort. I don't know what they can do against whatever we're dealing with, but it'd make me feel better."

Zéolie clutched his hand and gave it a squeeze as a blush stole across his face. "Thank you, Louis!"

Angelie smiled up at him. "Your heart's in the right place, Louis. You're right. She needs protection, but your men aren't what she needs. They couldn't protect Father Antoine, and they won't protect anyone else."

"Then what *does* she need?" Louis asked the nun.

"Camille," Zéolie answered.

Angelie would say no more as they rode back to the convent about how Camille could possibly protect Zéolie from a force that had already taken the lives of two formidable men. Louis began to doubt that the nun actually knew but didn't insult her by saying so. A dead grandmother seemed poor protection to Louis, but there was nothing he could say to sway the plans of the two women. His only hope was to convince Mother Micheaux to forbid the trip.

After saying his good-byes to Zéolie and Angelie, Louis made his way to the mother superior's office. Knocking softly on the half-opened door, he shifted his feet anxiously in the moment it took her to answer. "Come in, Louis," she called.

"Mother, I have a favor to ask of you," he began taking only a single step across the threshold.

"Of course, child, what is it?"

"After visiting Camille today, Zéolie and Angelie have their minds set on returning to her house to find answers." Mother Micheaux's pleasant expression darkened. He paused for a moment thinking she would immediately object but continued when she didn't. "I don't think it's a good idea at this point, but neither one'll listen to a word I've said. They'll listen to you if you forbid it."

Mother Micheaux sat back in her chair and folded her hands, resolute but. "I know you mean well, Louis," she said, "but I have to disagree with you this time. The answers are there. She must know what she's doing, or she wouldn't go back." She paused for a moment anticipating his next objection. "Julien's body has been removed from the house and the room sealed by police. Madame Marchon sent word this morning."

"It's not really that I fear upsetting her with seeing her father again," Louis began.

"I know," Mother Micheaux held up a hand to cut him off. "But there's nothing I can do. Truthfully, she's no safer here than at her own house. If that demon woman wants her, she'll find a way no matter where Zéolie is." Resigned to her decision, she folded her hands on the desk once more.

Louis was stunned by the mother superior's refusal to help keep Zéolie out of the house of horrors. "How can you say that? Nothing has happened to her here! Nothing has happened to anyone here. This must be a safe place for her. Somewhere just *has* to be!" Louis' emotions ran away with his mouth. His tear-filled eyes widened as he realized he just unleashed on the aging nun. "I—I'm sorry, Mother," he said quietly, hanging his head.

Mother Micheaux rose from her chair and put her hand on his arm. "There, now. It's alright. This has been hard on all of us and emotions are running high." She paused and continued softly, "Let her go home, Louis. She won't rest until she knows what's going on and if she thinks the answers are there, let her go home."

Louis wanted desperately to object, but the look on Mother Micheaux's face kept the words from forming. All he could manage was to nod slowly and mumble 'goodnight.'

CHAPTER
SIX

I t was another long night on the lumpy cot for Louis as he tried to sleep at the Ninth Ward precinct, which was fast becoming a second home for him. His superiors officially assigned him charge of Zéolie since she seemed to be most comfortable with him, which meant staying nearby. What little sleep did come was fraught with dreams of peaceful moments broken by explosions of shattered glass and screams from all around. Several times during the night, Louis bolted upright in bed, drenched in a cold sweat.

By morning, the rough night showed on his face. Tired sunken eyes seemed to have taken on more of a gray color than the deep ocean blue they had the day before. Sandy waves stuck up in every direction from the tossing and turning all night. "Good lord, man, you're a mess," he said to his reflection in the grimy precinct mirror.

After managing to tame his hair to some degree, he set out for the convent. There was still hope the women had come to their senses and changed their minds, but he seriously doubted it. All he could do now, was tag along and pray there was nothing to fear. A full patrol of guards remained around the Cheval house and nothing out of the ordinary had been reported since the priest's death. Even so, Louis didn't like it one bit.

As the carriage pulled up to the house on Dauphine, Zéolie shuddered. Memories and strange feelings of dread washed over her. Determined not to let them get the best of her, she steeled herself and walked up the front steps. Pausing with graceful fingers on the warm iron of the door handle, she took a slow deep breath. Angelie put a hand on Zéolie's arm to steady her as she turned the key in the lock. Metal scraped on metal as the bolt slid free. As the door swung in, the smell of roses and sage hit them like a wall of fragrance. The heady smell almost brought Zéolie to her knees.

Louis caught her elbow as she wavered and helped her over the threshold. "Are you sure you want to do this?" he asked gently.

Zéolie nodded and regained her composure, grateful for Louis' strength when she couldn't depend on her own. No, she wasn't sure, but she wasn't backing down now. Camille sent her back here for a reason.

"Close your eyes," Angelie coaxed. "Just be here for a moment. She'll guide you."

Louis hoped Angelie was talking about Camille and not the crazed voice. As he thought that, it struck him how strange things had become for him to hope that a nun was talking about a ghost rather than a disembodied voice.

Zéolie closed her dark eyes and tried to clear her cluttered mind. Flashes of memories darted in a convoluted frenzy before settling into a deep gray darkness. Laughter lingered at the edges of her thoughts, but she pushed it away. *Shut up*, she thought. *I don't have time for you now.* The voice let out one defiant cackle, then faded into a soft singsong again, barely there, but never gone.

Somewhere in the distance, images began to shimmer into focus in her mind. She was standing in a dust-covered room that smelled of old things and cedar. Looking around her, she saw trunks, crates, and an old rocking chair. Was it her attic? Slowly she opened her eyes. "I can see the attic. Maybe Camille thinks there's something we need to see there."

The trio made their way upstairs, passing the curious looks of the officers stationed throughout the house. Louis nodded acknowledgement at them but said nothing about why they were there. As they passed Julien's door, sealed with wax to keep anyone unauthorized from entering the crime scene, Zéolie thought how ridiculous the sealing wax was. If the voice wanted in, she damn sure wasn't going through the door. Steps away, a violent shudder seized Angelie. She looked for a moment at the door, crossed herself, then moved silently on. Zéolie and Louis exchanged looks, but neither said a word. If Angelie wanted to share what she felt, she would in her own time.

In a turn of the staircase, they came to the shorter wooden door of the entresol, the attic space between the first and second floors. Blazing heat of the Louisiana summers ruined anything kept in traditional attic spaces on the top stories of houses, so homes were built with the space between the floors. This kept anything placed there insulated by the house itself above and below. "I've never actually been in here," Zéolie said as she tried the handle on the entresol door. Nothing happened. "It's locked." She sighed leaning against the wall. It had always been locked. Why should today be any different?

"Do you have a key?" Angelie asked hopefully. Zéolie shook her head.

"Wait!" Louis said. "My brother and I used to sneak into our attic when we were little and make forts out of the trunks and boxes. My father finally locked us out when we broke an old clock that turned out to be a family heirloom. He hid the key in a groove on top of the doorframe. I was grown before I realized it was right there all along!" He reached his hand up and brought it back down with a handful of dust and an old brass key.

The key turned in the lock and the old mechanism made a grinding sound as it reluctantly released. Humidity over the years had warped the wooden door in its frame, which meant Louis had to put his full weight on it to push it open. A cloud of dust billowed out onto the landing, coating the wooden planks in a film of ashen gray.

Zéolie looked inside and saw her vision before her. She gasped and clutched Louis' hand. "It's just like what I saw downstairs!" Louis blushed at her touch and stepped in ahead of her to make sure it was safe before letting Zéolie go in.

Light streamed through the slats in a square set into the front wall that was supposed to serve as ventilation. It was too small to do much of that. Air hung thickly around them, close and warm. A layer of dust and time covered everything except for some crates set by the square vent that were covered in mildew. Clearly, the vent was better at letting in rain than fresh air. Most of the items were in trunks and crates stacked haphazardly around the attic room, dropped years before in whatever spot the servant carrying it up there felt like putting it. There was no rhyme or reason to anything.

"Where do we even start?" Zéolie asked looking at the possibilities in front of her.

"Over there," Angelie replied pointing to a far corner out of the light of the sunbeams and dancing dust fairies.

"Why there?" Zéolie asked.

Louis looked at Angelie to see if she had that odd look she wore when she was dealing with her mysterious talent. No, just her usual unemotional expression. He looked at the corner and quickly followed the nun's reasoning. "Because it seems to be the only place that has any care given to the way things are placed."

The corner was definitely different from the rest of the entresol. Boxes were stacked neatly, pressed up against the walls and as close to the far corner as they could possibly be. Huge cloths, that had once been white but were now yellowed with age, covered what appeared to be large picture frames and furniture. Louis pushed a few trunks out of the way to make room for the three of them to gather in the back corner to investigate.

Zéolie steadied her nerves and pulled one of the drapes away in a swirl of dust to reveal the rocking chair she had seen in her thoughts downstairs. Long fingers brushed gingerly along the aging wood. Another shiver of electricity danced up her spine. "I've never seen this chair before today. And, yet, it seems familiar. I don't understand."

"Keep searching, Zéolie," Angelie said quietly.

As they opened trunks, they found dresses, linens, and jewelry. With each item she touched, she felt the pulse of electricity. Not strong enough to hurt, but enough to get her attention. "These have to be my mother's things that Papa put up here when she died."

The voice, which had been absent since she walked into the house, whispered in her ear, "Good girl, cherie. Very good." A slow mocking chuckle, then nothing. The words startled her, but she said nothing. If Louis knew the voice was talking to her like it did the last time she was in the house, he'd make her leave.

"What's this?" Louis asked moving a trunk from in front of a large rectangle. "A painting maybe?"

Zéolie shrugged. "Take the drape off and let's see."

Louis pulled the drape away and Zéolie froze. Before her was a painting of a stunning young woman with black shining hair and deep dark eyes. Her mother. In her arms was a baby wearing a dress that looked familiar.

"Who is it, Zéolie?" Louis asked.

"I think it's my mother, but how is that me?" Zéolie looked closer at the little girl. She seemed to be about two months old. Too old to be her if what her father told her was true about her mother dying in childbirth. The baby had little dark curls, and dark eyes like her mother. "It must be me, but it couldn't be." Zéolie's fingers reached toward the baby on the painting but stopped just shy of touching it. "The dress. I know that dress."

Zéolie spun on her heel and raced out of the entresol. Louis and Angelie followed hard on her heels to her bedroom on the second floor where they found Zéolie standing in the center of her room staring at a doll in a tiny chair in the corner wearing the same dress as the infant in the portrait. The doll in the dress connected her to her mother. As the realization of what this all meant began to sink in, Zéolie's head swam and her stomach rolled.

"It's me," she whispered. "I'm the baby in the portrait. It was all lies." She turned slowly to face Angelie and Louis, pushing down the wave of nausea. Tears glistened on long black lashes. "I didn't want to believe what Mother Micheaux told you. I wanted what Papa told me to be true." As the realization that her father kept secrets from her washed over Zéolie, fresh pain pricked her heart. The laugh in her mind rumbled deep and menacing. "He lied to me. Papa *lied* to me!" Words choked her as she forced them out. "She didn't die when I was born like he said, but I've seen the date on her tomb. It's my birthday. Why would he lie about when she died? I don't understand. I don't understand any of it." Zéolie sank to the floor, stunned and staring into the space in front of her.

Louis knelt beside her and put his arm around her shoulder. So strong moments before as she searched for answers, now she was small and scared. "Your father must have had his reasons, Zéolie." Turning her face into his chest, she broke down in sobs that shook her whole body. Holding her in that moment, he forgot the reasons he shouldn't have the feelings he had for her. All that mattered in his world was her pain and the ache in his heart that he couldn't take it away.

Leaving Louis to comfort Zéolie, Angelie slipped out to speak to one of the officers. After a few minutes, she returned to find Zéolie recovered from her shock and dabbing at her eyes with Louis' handkerchief. "There's somewhere else we need to go," Angelie said flatly.

CHAPTER

SEVEN

Walls seemed to whisper as Zéolie, Louis, and Angelie passed through the entrance to St. Louis Cemetery at the edge of the Quarter. The dead seemed restless in their tombs even in the quiet and dappled sunshine that surrounded them. Angelie ran her hand along the small brick and plaster arches in the wall mouthing silent prayers as if trying to soothe the spirits within.

The dead lay ensconced in layers of tombs within the walls themselves, one on top of the other, sealed with bricks and a layer of plaster. Some were temporary residences of the corpses who had died before the diocese's mandate of "a year and a day" passed. The aboveground tombs inside the walls were erected to house entire families and save the precious solid ground in the city, but with outbreaks of yellow fever, some families were losing members faster than they could bury them. The wealthy had built crypts with more than one layer for such occasions. Others had only the one space that was reused over and over. When someone died, the body was laid to rest and the tomb sealed. The Church required that the dead be left at peace for a full year and a day before the bones could be moved to the rear of the crypt and the slab reused. Over the year, the Louisiana heat would turn the tomb into a crematorium, reducing the contents to dust. If a family member died within this time, they were held in a temporary tomb in the cemetery walls. Given their transient residence, Zéolie could understand their restlessness.

There was seemingly no order to the cemetery, and it began to feel like an eerie maze of marble and brick. Tall monuments would jut up above the smaller tombs and serve as navigational points. Otherwise, the tombs were relatively low. Most weren't very wide at the front but would go back from the path deep enough to hold a wooden coffin in front of the sacks of ancestral remains in the back of the crypt. Paths would turn into bogs in wet weather and become almost impassable. Thankfully, the paths were dry and dusty, baked by the Louisiana sun. They had to work quickly, though. Large white clouds were building above their heads. Rain was on the way.

Zéolie was a child the last time she went to the tomb of her mother and wasn't sure where it was in the maze before her. "She's here somewhere, but I don't know where it is. I—I never visit here." A pang of guilt stung her. A good daughter would have paid homage to her dead mother. Zéolie felt nothing for the woman she never knew and visiting Solène's grave hadn't been important to her.

"Can you feel it like you felt Camille's?" Louis asked Zéolie.

Angelie shook her head. "Not if I'm right."

"About what?" he asked.

Angelie just shrugged and went back to her prayers for the dead.

Louis looked at Zéolie. "What does she mean?"

"I have no idea. I can't hear the voice. You'd think she'd have something to say about this." She glanced over at the two increasingly impatient men who had been assigned by the Church to help them with their mission.

"Well, we won't find her by standing around wondering where she is." Louis shoved his hands in his pockets, picked a path, and started walking. Zéolie followed hoping something would speak to her as they searched.

Passing the different tombs, Zéolie's gaze wandered from the names to the trinkets and flowers placed in front of some of the graves. Flowers for husbands and wives, infant toys left by grieving mothers. Other graves had unusual items like small half-drunk bottles of alcohol. Zéolie imagined someone sitting in the dark sharing a drink with the spirit of a friend and leaving the rest of the bottle for them. Other things like candle stubs, cigars, Voodoo charms, and coins lay against the stone crypts as protection for the dead. *Or protection against them*, Zéolie thought.

After weaving through several rows, the group eventually found themselves standing in front of the Cheval family's tomb. Tall and narrow, the white concrete-coated tomb stretched away from the path slightly further than the length of a coffin. On either side, on the ground slab that looked like a low step up into the tomb, were two carved marble vases with polished stone flowers. A peaked front showed the activity of a recent death. The smaller marble placard on the front had been removed to be engraved for her father leaving the layer of mortar that covered the brick exposed. Thinking about why the marble was missing brought a lump to Zéolie's throat and quickened her pulse. Standing amid the tombs and statues knowing why she came, she suddenly felt very small and unsure of herself.

The graveyard workers shuffled their feet impatiently as Zéolie drank in the sight of the tomb where her mother lay. She still couldn't believe Angelie thought they should be doing this. How was the dust of her mother's bones going to solve anything?

Folding her hands at her waist to still their shaking, she took a deep breath. "I'm ready," she said finally. "Open it."

The uneasy men began to chisel at the mortar that sealed the slab in front of the crypt. With every swing of the hammer and ring of the chisel against the stone, Zéolie trembled. Nothing about what was happening seemed real. This was insane. She was insane. No sane person hears voices and opens graves unnecessarily. Minutes passed that seemed like hours. Maybe it had been hours. Zéolie didn't know anymore. Time seemed to yawn out in front of her pulling farther and farther away with each swing of the hammers. What the hell were they doing here?

Louis paced around the tombs looking for something, anything, nothing. Angelie knelt in prayer and hadn't moved in a long time. Zéolie just stood there in front of the crypt watching shards of mortar flying from the chisel.

After what seemed like an eternity, a graveyard worker stood and wiped his brow. "You might wanna stand back, m'amselle. I'd hate for you to get hurt if it falls when we move the brick."

"Of course," Zéolie replied stepping well out of the way. Louis heard the hammers stop and came to stand next to her. Angelie got to her feet and took Zéolie's hand in hers.

Another eternity passed as the men inched the bricks away from the crypt. Cuts strategically made pull the brick wall, sealing the tomb out in as few pieces as possible since they knew they were just going to have to seal it again. As the first section was removed, Zéolie expected a terrible stench of death to come wafting out, but there was nothing. Hesitant steps inched her closer to the gaping tomb. It took all of her resolve to look inside. She had seen enough gruesomeness in the past few days. Zéolie wasn't sure she could take any more, but she had to look inside. They needed to see Solène's bones to know what had happened to her. Somehow, Angelie knew some of the puzzle would be answered here. Zéolie held her breath against the dust and fear and peered into the darkness of the crypt. She expected a skeleton. She saw a rose.

The delicate flower rested on the slab where her mother's body should have been. There should have been remnants of a wooden coffin and a skeleton. If nothing else, the intense New Orleans heat should have at least left a pile of ash after the wood and flesh disintegrated in the stone crypt. There was nothing. No sign that the tomb had ever been inhabited. The slab bore no more dust than the removal of the bricks would have left. And the rose bore no sign of age. It was a deep velvety black rosebud, barely opened.

The voice in her head that was silent since their arrival at the cemetery began a deep slow laugh, dark and menacing. Fear shot through her like a bolt of lightning. Zéolie began to tremble so violently that Louis had to hold her shoulders to keep her upright. Angelie dropped back to her knees in a quick murmuring prayer. This time, though, she hadn't crossed herself, but the others were too preoccupied to notice. At the sight of the rose, the grave workers fled, swearing and white with fear.

"*Foolish girl!*" the voice boomed above their heads. Echoes reverberated off the tombs, scattered and terrifying. "And I had such hopes for you."

Zéolie wheeled around and faced Louis whose fingers suddenly dug into Zéolie's arms. Wide frightened eyes told her Louis heard the voice, too.

Wind whipped around them stinging their faces with graveyard dust and shards of mortar. Tiny droplets of blood began to appear on skin they couldn't shield from the onslaught. Zéolie tried to cover her face with her hands, but soon they were bleeding, too. A cold sweat broke out all over her body as electricity surged in the air around her. "Stop it!" she shrieked above the din of roaring laughter and whipping wind. "Enough of this!"

Instead of stopping the storm, the ground began to rumble beneath their feet and the maniacal laughter became a furious roar. "Don't you *dare* defy me, child!" Zéolie's hands flew instinctively to cover her ears. Cracks began to form in the sides of the crypt, streaking across the smooth stone like a spider web, yet the rose on the slab lay still and fresh, unaffected by the raging all around it. "You won't find your mother here!" the voice snarled.

"Solène," Zéolie whispered as understanding dawned on her. "The voice. It's Solène."

Angelie began to rock back and forth, never ceasing her murmuring.

"And *you*! You foolish little nun," the voice spat. "You should have known better, wretch. Didn't Camille teach you *anything*?"

Angelie's lips stopped moving as her eyes snapped open. Hands no longer clasped in prayer pushed her body up from the dusty jagged ground. Zéolie stared wide-eyed at Angelie, who was on her feet now walking towards the crypt with slow deliberate steps. "Yes," Angelie whispered, "she did." The nun's small white hand stretched out towards the rose.

"You keep your filthy hands away from that rose!" demanded the voice. The ground rocked under Angelie's feet and she stumbled onto the broken mortar. Louis stepped forward to help her, but Zéolie held him back, not wanting him to incur the wrath of the voice. Undeterred, Angelie stood up and steadied herself. Her hand flashed out and grabbed the rose, thorns digging deep into her palm and fingers. Deep crimson blood streamed down Angelie's wrist and pooled at the cuff of her habit, but still she clutched the black rose as if her life depended on it.

Zéolie and Louis looked on stunned as the rose began to wither and die in the nun's hand. Leaves that were fresh and green a moment earlier, turned brown and withered. Petals aged and began to drop off at Angelie's feet. She put one foot out and, with the toe of her shoe, ground a petal into the dirt. "*You'll pay for that, you little wench!*" the voice screamed.

With one final thunderclap of rage, the storm of wind and roaring stopped leaving them in dead silence. Angelie smiled sheepishly at Zéolie, went ashen white, and fainted as Louis dove to catch her.

Zéolie and Louis managed to revive Angelie somewhat, but the experience left the nun in a state of catharsis. She was able to shakily stand, but her eyes remained glazed and staring blankly ahead of her. Not wanting to risk her safety on the uneven pathways, Louis scooped Angelie up and carried her to the carriage outside the cemetery walls. She would make no sound, answer no questions.

Soon, the carriage returned to the Ursuline convent in the Ninth Ward and Angelie was taken to her room. "Go on to the parlor," instructed Mother Micheaux hastily. "You have visitors, Zéolie. I'll see to Angelie." With a squeeze of Zéolie's hand, she hurried down the corridor with her habit billowing behind her.

Louis looped Zéolie's arm through his to support her as they walked the hallway to the parlor. Exhaustion and fear churned in Zéolie's gut. "I'm not sure I can stand to see anyone right now," she said wearily.

"There aren't many people who know you're here, and those are close to you. This might be just what you need right now."

Zéolie half-smiled up at him and patted his arm. "Maybe."

Lamps had been lit in the parlor to stave off the darkness from the gathering storm outside. A soft golden glow spilled out into the hallway from the parlor entry. It did seem inviting to her as Zéolie steadied herself to face whoever had come. Stepping through the threshold, she found herself immediately in the arms of Lisette with Celeste grinning at her from a few steps behind her sister.

"Zéolie!" Lisette squealed squeezing her friend even tighter.

"Lisette, you'll hurt her," Celeste chided. "Let her go, you ninny."

Lisette turned and stuck her tongue out at her older sister but did as she was told. Madame Marchon shot a look of disgust at Lisette, who immediately put her tongue back in and sat sheepishly on the settee. The older woman came forward, taking Zéolie's hands and led her to an armchair. "Sit down, cherie. You've clearly been through a lot. Sister," Madame Marchon called to the young novice who was playing hostess to the women in the absence of Mother Micheaux.

"Yes, madame?" the sister asked.

"Would you please get some warm water and towels to clean these wounds?"

"Of course, madame." With a slight nod the sister sped off to carry out the instructions.

In the mental chaos, Zéolie completely forgot all of the tiny cuts from the mortar. "Thank you. You always know what needs doing." Lisette sat at Zéolie's feet and held her hand while Celeste rested on the arm of the chair with her hand gently on Zéolie's shoulder.

"How in the world did you get yourself in this condition? And you, too, Louis?" Worry settled in the fine lines of Madame Marchon's face as she inspected Zéolie's bloody hands.

Zéolie shook her head slowly. "I'm afraid it's a long story and I don't think you'd believe me if I told you. I'm not sure I believe it myself."

"Try me," Madame Marchon insisted.

In spite of her fear that her oldest friends would think she was a lunatic, Zéolie began to relate the strange events of the past few days with Louis filling in gaps when words failed her. The sister returned with the water and cloths and helped Madame Marchon tend to the cuts and scrapes on Zéolie and Louis's hands and faces. As Zéolie reached the events from earlier in the day, Mother Micheaux appeared at the doorway.

"You're just in time, Mother," Louis said. "We've been filling in Madame Marchon and the ladies about the last two days, and we've just gotten to what happened at the cemetery."

"How's Angelie?" Zéolie asked wincing as Madame Marchon cleaned a particularly deep cut on her cheek.

Mother Micheaux shook her head. "No change, but she's lying down now under the watchful eye of one of the elder sisters. Whatever you all went through at the tomb took a toll on her in more ways than just cuts and dust."

"All I can tell you is what Louis and I saw and heard, but to really know what she went through, we'll need to hear from Angelie. There was something happening only she could understand." Zéolie related in detail everything that she and Louis experienced, but she had no idea what else was happening to Angelie or how she knew to take the rose out of the tomb to end the raging.

"And she said nothing of it all the way home?" Mother Micheaux asked.

Louis shook his head. "Nothing. She hasn't said a word since. It's almost like she's somewhere else."

"Like a trance or something?" asked Lisette. Celeste shushed her sister, but Zéolie nodded.

"Yes, like a trance," Zéolie replied. "I don't understand any of what happened today. When I try to put it together, it just doesn't make sense." Aching muscles and stinging wounds began to wear on her. Zéolie leaned back in the chair and closed her eyes against the pain and exhaustion.

For a long moment, they all sat in silence, each sorting through the events of the day in their own thoughts. After a moment, Louis asked, "Mother, could I trouble you for some paper, pen, and some ink? I think if we write down what we know, we can get a better picture of things." Tightness in his voice revealed strain he was trying desperately to hide.

Mother Micheaux nodded at Sister Mary Michael who hurried to get the things he asked for. "Good idea, Louis. We should look at the evidence like any good police officer would."

With a slight groan as he pulled his stiff muscles out of the chair, Louis brought a small table over to where he had been sitting. Zéolie brought a lamp for him that was on the table beside her and set it down. "Thank you, Zéolie," he said softly with a tired crooked smile. A soft pink blush stole over her pale cheeks and her beauty in that moment almost got the best of him. His heart tightened in his chest and his hand trembled slightly as he turned the lamp up. *She's just a victim in an investigation,* Louis lied to himself again and tried desperately to focus on the task at hand.

Madame Marchon stood and paced the room in thought. "I'd say we need to write down everything Zéolie was told by her father, but it seems we can't count on that information," she said. "Sorry, cherie, I mean no offense, of course."

Zéolie smiled wanly. "None taken. I agree with you." Her mother's voice in her head that had been relatively quiet since the outburst at the cemetery began to chuckle. Zéolie put her hands to the sides of her head and winced.

Louis' eyes narrowed. He was quickly learning what that look on her face meant. "What is it, Zéolie? What's she saying?"

"She's laughing at us." Zéolie threw her head back and groaned. "Shut up, you despicable woman!" Laughter grew louder and then faded into the recesses again.

Slowly, the group began to talk through the events and discoveries since the death of Julien Cheval. Louis took notes, crossing things out that were no longer true with the new information from the last two days. Added to the list was the history of Zéolie's mother and grandmother as Mother Micheaux told them the first night. Eventually, Louis sat back in his chair as the darkness and rain began to fall. The list of facts was complete, at least as far as they knew at this point in the game. Anything that was speculation was placed on a separate page. Louis looked at the evening's work with satisfaction. As a police officer, it was a good start. As a realist, he couldn't believe some of the things he had written down as facts in the case.

"So, let me get this straight," began Celeste. "Your grandmother was a witch, your mother may not be dead, and you and the nun hear voices. Have I got the gist of it?"

"Well, yes," Zéolie replied.

"Alright, then," Celeste said and sat down on the settee satisfied with her own understanding. "None of it makes any sense and that makes perfect sense to everyone."

Zéolie knew Celeste was right in her own flippant way. None of it made any rational sense. When Celeste summed it all up like that, it did sound a bit ludicrous. Zéolie sat for a while with her head in her hands feeling the full weight of her situation. Her perfect little world collapsed in a matter of days and her sanity had apparently gone with the rest of it. Voices, missing corpses, strange paintings, and bizarre murders. This was not the life she knew and grew up with, but now she was starting to see that the life she thought she knew was all make-believe. Now that she had the truth, she was struggling to come to terms with it.

Mother Micheaux broke the silence that hung over the room. "Come," she said standing and smoothing her black robes. "It's late and everyone's exhausted from all this. You need to get some rest before the service tomorrow."

Zéolie's head jerked up. Tomorrow. Her father's funeral. She had completely lost track of the time. "Oh, no. That's right!" She turned frantic eyes to Madame Marchon. "I'm so sorry! I haven't helped you with anything."

"It's all right, cherie," Madame Marchon said placing a reassuring hand on Zéolie's shoulder. "I've seen to everything and I'll make sure you aren't bothered with questions. Louis'll be there as well as a dozen officers in plain clothes...just in case." Madame Marchon kissed her on the cheek and gestured for the girls to go. Lisette and Celeste hugged Zéolie as they followed their mother out of the parlor. Lisette sniffled and wiped a tear as she turned to wave at her friend. Celeste tried to appear less emotional, but even she couldn't hide the tears glistening in her eyes as Mother Micheaux led them out.

"Poor things," Zéolie sighed. "This is too much for them to take in all at once."

"They'll be fine. It's you I'm worried about," Louis said softly. He knelt beside the chair and took her hand in his. Her fingers were cold and trembling. As strong as she appeared on the outside, inside she was a torrent of emotions. "I promise I'll do all I can to protect you. I..."

"I know," Zéolie answered softly.

Louis blinked at her. She knew? How could she know? "You know?" he asked.

"I know you won't let anything happen to me if you can stop it," she replied. *And I know you love me*, she thought.

"Of—of course," Louis stammered. A blush stole across his face as he stood. "I should let you get some rest. You've got a long day ahead of you tomorrow." He kissed the hand he held letting his lips linger on her soft skin longer than he intended.

Zéolie smiled. "Goodnight, Louis." As she stood to go, she rose to her tip-toes and kissed him on the cheek letting her lips linger longer than she had intended.

CHAPTER
EIGHT

The morning of Julien Cheval's funeral dawned with spectacular beauty. Wisps of clouds on the horizon gleamed with pinks, purples, and sparkling silver edges. Sunbeams shot out over the tops of the clouds in shimmering soft white. Behind them, a pale blue sky. The shining sunrise was a stark contrast to the heavily veiled figure in mourning blacks in the convent garden.

Zéolie stood in the courtyard looking through a black gauze veil at the sky. She had always looked at the dawn as a new beginning, but today was the dawning of the end of her time with her father. A single tear trickled down her cheek and dropped on her sleeve. Closing her eyes, she could almost feel him standing beside her, his strength and protection within reach. "I still need you, Papa. I always will." In the depths of her mind Solène chuckled, but said nothing.

Raising the dark veil, Zéolie drank in the beauty of the sunrise and the heady fragrance of the courtyard flowers willing the peace of the morning to infuse the depths of her soul and the far reaches of her mind. Angelie would have loved this moment, she thought. Another pang shot through her heart as she thought of the nun staring mutely into space. With a sigh, she lowered her veil and went back inside.

She wanted to see Angelie before she went to the funeral. Surely there would be some good news this time that she could cling to as she dealt with what was to come. Since the cemetery, the nun had been completely cathartic. The sisters caring for her had instructions to tell Zéolie the instant anything changed in Angelie's condition, no matter how slight, but no one had come.

Zéolie was a statuesque shadow walking through the convent corridors. Only the rustling of her skirts gave her away as anything more real. Nuns who passed bowed their heads and lowered their eyes respectfully, but what she really needed was their reassuring smiles.

The door to Angelie's room was slightly ajar, but Zéolie knocked anyway. Her glove muffled the sound and she wasn't sure if anyone heard it. Just as her hand raised to knock again, Sister Anne Marie opened the door.

"How is she, Sister?" Zéolie asked in a whisper.

The nun bowed her head and lowered her eyes like the others. "No change, mademoiselle."

"Can I see her?"

"Of course. I'll be just outside if you need me." Sister Anne Marie held the door open for Zéolie before slipping into the corridor.

Zéolie crossed the tiny cell to Angelie's bedside and knelt down. The small figure of her friend didn't move as Zéolie took the nun's hand in hers. Thin icy fingers lay limply in her palm even though the room was warm. No trace of the strange and wonderful young woman she'd come to know. Blankness. Emptiness. "I'm so sorry, Angelie. This is all my fault, and I don't know how to fix it...how to help you." Strength and words failing her, Zéolie laid her head on the bed in a wordless prayer. The weight of her grief and worry were almost more than she could carry anymore. Words eluded her, even as she tried to recall prayers she'd said a hundred times or more. There was no room for words in her heart on a morning like this. Zéolie gave Angelie's hand a slight squeeze and stood to go. For a long moment, she looked at the shell of her friend, staring straight ahead, blinking slowly. Tearing herself away, she nodded to Sister Anne Marie as she slipped back out into the corridor.

Madame Marchon's carriage sent to take her to the cathedral had a simple black wreath on the small door. Heavy black curtains were drawn shut so prying eyes couldn't gawk at the tragic heiress as she made her way to the funeral. All the mourning proprieties were in place thanks to the careful planning of Madame Marchon, but Zéolie wasn't ready to grieve her father just yet. Not until she had answers. Until then, there was work to do. Mourning could wait.

Mother Micheaux sat across from her in the dark stuffy carriage. Rays of sunlight snuck around the curtain edges and danced along the carriage walls as it rumbled through the city streets. The mother superior spent the journey deep in prayer with her thin, wrinkled hands working through the worn wooden beads of the rosary at her waist. Zéolie spent it deep in thought picking at a thread on her glove. She had been to funerals before, but always as a guest of the family. Zéolie had no idea what she was supposed to do as the daughter of the deceased.

As she rode through the city, Zéolie tried not to listen to the ramblings of the voice in her mind that was wearing on her sanity. Solène made up idiotic poems about rotting corpses and the creatures that dispose of them, reciting them with great enthusiasm.

A handsome feast for maggots and flies,
Vultures and crows fight over his eyes,
Insides out with the point of a knife,
All for the love of a guttersnipe.

By the time the carriage reached the cathedral, she had put the poems to music. Her mother was thoroughly entertained by the burial of her father and it was sickening.

Getting through the funeral mass was going to be difficult enough with Solène's constant babble and singing. God forbid she decide to lash out. Zéolie couldn't face down her mother without Angelie and Louis. Not today.

THE CARRIAGE SLOWED to a stop at the front of the cathedral and Zéolie peeked through the curtain. A crowd of strangers gathered in the Place D'Armes and police were stationed there to keep the mass from pressing any closer to the church. Opportunists wove their way through the press of bodies hawking their wares and selling them from baskets they carried. On the far side closest to the river was a man in stocks that seemed more concerned with the grim festivities than his personal condition. In one corner of the square, there was a scuffle over position that threatened to escalate until a police officer intervened. A morbid carnival.

"It's madness," Zéolie whispered.

"It's disgusting," Mother Micheaux declared as she gathered her robes. "Duck your head and go quickly into the doors. There are officers to escort you."

"Louis?"

Mother Micheaux shook her head. "I don't think so, cherie, but he's here somewhere."

An officer opened the carriage door and nodded at the women. "This way, mademoiselle. Quickly." As he helped her out of the carriage, Zéolie could feel the wave of bodies behind her surge forward. Whistles and shouts from the police ordered them back. Above her head, the cathedral bell tolled slowly as if to remind the unruly throng that this was a somber occasion.

Zéolie always loved St. Louis Cathedral with its whitewashed façade that gleamed in the sunlight. The hexagonal towers on each side rose to the heavens with their bell-shaped roofs and flanked the newer center tower that held the clock and *Victoire*, the Parisian bell that now rang for her father. As much as she loved the place, she could not stop to gaze at its majesty today.

She arrived later than the mourners by design. Madame Marchon wanted her to be able to enter the service as it began to avoid questions and trivialities from well-wishers. The crowd in the square paled in comparison to the gathering inside. All three sections of pews were packed with people ranging from the highest of society to the common businessmen of the Quarter and their families. Mothers fanned themselves and hushed restless children. Men dabbed at their foreheads with handkerchiefs or shirt cuffs.

Zéolie stood at the back of the beautifully tiled aisle that led to the front altar where a priest stood waiting for her. He wore formal white robes and held his Bible in both hands at his waist. How she wished it was Father Antoine at the other end of the expanse between them. She closed her eyes and imagined how she always thought she would be walking down this same aisle one day: dressed in gilded white, a bouquet of irises in one hand, and her arm looped through her father's strong arm. Instead, she found herself in mourning blacks walking alone down the same aisle to where her father lay at the base of the massive altar in a closed casket.

"One foot in front of the other," she told herself. "One step at a time." Fabric rustled as the mourners noticed her presence in the back of the church. Whispered conversation silenced and the only sound was the baleful organ above her head. Slowly, she made the long walk to the front of the basilica to take her place in the front pew. A somber specter gliding down the aisle. Each step felt heavier than the last. Each step brought her closer to good-bye. As she walked, she noticed a glint of light on one of the statues. Joan of Arc. The saint stood determined in her silver armor with her banner waving. 'Steel yourself for the battle, Zéolie,' she seemed to say. 'Courage. You are not alone.' With a nod to the statue, Zéolie continued to the altar.

As she got closer to her father's coffin, Solène began singing her repulsive songs of death and decay.

A preist, a nun, and some communion wine
On a fine spring day had a real good time

By Christmas time, they burned in Hell
While a baby sleeps forever in the convent well.

She worked the words into the music from the organ. Rich tones in minor keys rang through the cathedral lulling the mourners into a sense of reverence and prayer. Those seated in the pews were mercifully spared the hideous details of Solène's gruesome songs.

Zéolie stood at the foot of the altar steps and gazed at the closed casket before her. The wood shone with polish in the light streaming down from the gilded candelabra. Sealed inside was something that only barely resembled her father. Instinctively, she knelt before the altar and casket then crossed herself with trembling black-gloved hands. Tidal waves of memories flooded her as her knees touched the ground, crushing the breath out of her as she held back the surge of tears threatening to break through the dam of decorum and strength. Her broken heart lodged itself in her throat as if reaching for her father who lay mangled under a shroud of gleaming wood. Fighting against the weight of grief pushing her down, Zéolie stood and placed her shaking hand on the coffin lid before slowly turning away from it and taking her place in the front pew.

With a gesture from the priest, the congregation stood in unison and the funeral mass began. As they rose, a cannon fired outside signaling the start of the service and startling Zéolie. The first hymn faded into the prayers and liturgy. She was merely going through the motions, hearing little of what was said and sung over the din in her head. Solène was having a wonderful time cackling and singing along with the priest.

Zéolie tried focusing her attention on the paintings and statues in front of her, but even that brought commentary from Solène. The huge Rococo mural above the altar told the story of King Louis IX of France and his saintliness, but Solène amused herself by telling Zéolie lewd tales of what the saint was really like behind closed doors. Even the statues of the Christian virtues of Faith, Hope, and Charity were not immune to Solène's bawdiness. It seemed wherever

Zéolie tried to focus her attention, her mother could twist it into something vile.

The mass continued with prayers and hymns celebrating the life of the deceased and his victory over sin and death. Painfully generic to Zéolie who thought about the vibrant strong man she knew. He was so much more than what the priest said he was. So much more life and depth. And so many more secrets.

Her mother's antics passed unnoticed by anyone but Zéolie throughout the service. Toward the end of the mass, it was time for the Eucharist. As the organ played, the Marchon women, at Zéolie 's request in a break with the all-male tradition of the Church, brought the holy gifts of bread, water, and wine to the front of the altar and stood to the side of the priest as he performed the rites of communion. As the ritual came to an end, he offered bread and wine to the women. First was Madame Marchon. The priest placed the wafer on her tongue and then she took the wine chalice. She drank a sip, crossed herself and stepped aside. Lisette did the same.

Last was Celeste. A wafer was placed on her tongue and she lifted the chalice to her lips. Taking a small sip, she made a move to lower the chalice but couldn't. The cup refused to leave her mouth. Celeste's long slender fingers clawed at the cup trying to force it away from her face, but it was futile. Eyes flashed wild with panic and fear. Crimson wine rushed into Celeste's mouth choking her and pouring down her face onto her dress and the floor, then began to pool at her feet. It gushed from the cup in impossible volumes as the girl struggled to free herself. Gasps and cries from the crowd in the sanctuary became shrieks of terror as the poor girl choked and strangled.

The priest sprang into action trying to cast the demon from the cup and Zéolie ran to the aid of her friend. *"Damn you, woman!"* Grief and rage surged through Zéolie as she screamed into the empty space around Celeste. *"Release her!"* A hard slap from nowhere landed on Zéolie's face and sent her reeling backwards into the arms of Lisette and Madame Marchon.

"*Drink up, girl!*" rang out through the cathedral. Faces in the pews searched frantically and hopelessly for the owner of the voice no longer raging only in Zéolie's mind. Celeste was drowning in wine as she struggled to spit out as much as she could. "Come on, now, child." Solène chided. "You always wanted to have a good time. Well, *here it is!*"

Terrified mourners began screaming and spilling out of the church adding to the chaos outside. Seeing the panic from the mourners fleeing the church, the curious crowd that had been dispersed by police during the service quickly returned. Officers surged into the sanctuary against the sea of bodies trying to get outside and away from whatever force attacked the poor girl on holy ground. Once inside, the officers found Celeste convulsing on the floor covered in red wine. One officer raced outside to find a doctor to tend to the girl, while others did what they could for her, which was useless at best. The rest tried to calm the other women and determine what happened. Laughter rang through the church as Celeste's convulsions ebbed. The echo still hung in the air as the doctor arrived on the scene to tend to the traumatized girl.

It was then that the priest finally was able to turn his attention to Zéolie. His once-white robes were splashed in red. "I'm sorry, child. I'm so sorry. I did all that I knew to do... I've—I've never seen anything like it."

"Please don't apologize, Father. There's not much any of us could do against a force like this."

The priest led her aside out of earshot of the attending physician. "Do you know what you're dealing with here?"

Zéolie nodded. "Yes, but not completely. She's dangerous, Father. The less you know about this, the safer you are."

She knew the priest was considering the unexplained death of Father Antoine as he looked levelly at her. "Then, I will offer my prayers and say no more. If you need anything..."

Giving him a wan smile, she replied, "Thank you, Father." He nodded and went to see about Celeste.

"Zéolie!" Louis called down the aisle of the church. "What happened?"

She rushed down the aisle to him and stopped just short of falling into his arms. Shaking, she explained, "Louis! It was Solène. She's been taunting me all morning with repulsive songs and stories, laughing at me and everyone here. I thought she was just amusing herself tormenting me. But then- then she went after Celeste during communion. She tried to drown her with the wine. And she nearly managed to do it, too. I honestly don't know what stopped her."

Louis knelt beside Celeste. She was soaked in wine and sweat but seemed to be physically fine for the most part. The poor girl was badly shaken and clearly intoxicated even though sacramental wine is diluted with holy water. "After what she went through, the drunkenness might be a welcome thing to keep the details of the whole experience cloudy in her memory," Louis said.

Other officers had begun collecting information for the report, which would be as ineffective as the one from the Cheval house, so he focused his efforts on getting the women taken care of and safely transported home. Mother Micheaux had been standing sentinel at the front doors of the cathedral counseling those who were terrorized by the scene at the altar but passed the responsibilities to other clergy so she could escort Zéolie back to the convent. "They're in good hands, cherie. There's nothing more you can do. We need to get you out of here without being seen." The mother superior took Zéolie down the corridors to the rectory where the body of Father Antoine lay awaiting his burial. A lump lodged itself in the back of Zéolie's throat as she looked down at Father Antoine and thought of what Solène was capable of and what Celeste narrowly escaped. Zéolie and Mother Micheaux paused and crossed themselves before continuing to a back entrance that opened onto a side alley. With all the commotion in the square, no one would notice her exit. An officer at the back door had a carriage pulled up as close to the door as possible allowing Zéolie to climb in virtually unseen. With curtains shut against gawking eyes, the carriage tore back through the French Quarter to the convent.

Mother Micheaux led the weary girl into the parlor and poured her a glass of brandy to steady her shaking hands. Curtains had been drawn against the heat of the day and lamps lit. "Sit down and drink this. You need it." Mother Micheaux smiled and handed the brandy to Zéolie. "I need to go let the sisters know we're home safe. It amazes me how quickly word travels in this city and I don't want them worried." With that, she left to go find one of the senior nuns.

Just as she laid her head back on the chair cushion and closed her eyes, a young nun rushed into the parlor out of breath. "Mademoiselle Cheval! She said it was you coming in!"

"Who did?" Zéolie asked.

"Angelie! She's asking for you. She won't talk to anyone else."

Zéolie jumped up and raced out of the room with the young nun hard on her heels. "Send word to Officer Saucier," she called over her shoulder. The novice skidded on the wood floor, then ran the other direction to carry out Zéolie's order.

It wasn't until she was at the threshold of Angelie's room that Zéolie slowed her pace. After all she had been through, she didn't want to burst in on Angelie and frighten her. Breathless, Zéolie pushed the door open and found Angelie sitting on her bed with her legs gathered up under her habit. Sunlight from the open window streamed in rays onto the floor. Angelie's face was ashen, but her eyes regained their light. A weak smile crept over the nun's face as she saw Zéolie's figure in the doorway. "Zéolie, are you alright?"

"Don't worry about me. How are *you* doing?"

"A lot better now," she answered with a shrug. "I'm sorry I missed the funeral this morning. I-I wanted to go, but-"

Zéolie cut her off. "Nonsense. You needed rest after what happened. I completely understand."

Angelie shook her head and dropped her eyes to her lap. "It wasn't that. She wouldn't release me. She—she held me here."

"Who?' Slowly it began to dawn on Zéolie who Angelie meant, and her gut tightened. "*Solène?*"

Angelie nodded weakly. "I tried to break free of her, but I couldn't. It was too much." Color drained from her face as she talked. "She's so *powerful*. At the crypt, she was so strong, and I was afraid she'd kill you for opening the grave. Turning her wrath on me was all I could think of to do, but—" Tears tumbled down her face, splashing onto the black robe that swirled around her small frame.

Zéolie sat on the edge of the bed and put her arms around Angelie. Never since all of this began had she seen much emotion from nun. Until now, she'd seemed immune to the madness of it all. Something had broken in her at the cemetery.

Moments passed as fear and relief wracked Angelie's body until finally her sobs and breathing calmed. "There's so much rage in her," Angelie whispered at last. "More than I've ever felt in anyone. Such force behind how she directs it!"

"Others who got in her way died for it. Do you have any idea why she spared you?" Zéolie asked gently.

Angelie's tear-stained eyes looked up at Zéolie. "Solène didn't spare me. At least, she didn't want to. She threw as much of her rage at me that she could, but there was something shielding me. It was as if I was watching her attack through a pane of glass. I could see what she was trying to do, but she couldn't touch me. That only made her angrier, but no matter what she did, I was protected."

"But how?" Zéolie asked. "How did you shield yourself from her?"

"It wasn't me."

Zéolie looked hard at Angelie as the answer to it all came to her. "Camille?"

Angelie nodded. "When I was kneeling there, I knew prayer wasn't what we needed. I was on my knees begging Camille to step in, and she did. It was as if Camille was the window I was watching everything through."

"What did you see?"

"Nothing, everything. I can't explain it. It was like watching the raging of a distant storm. Swirling and crashing, but always just out of reach. Swelling and churning like the sea in a hurricane..." Angelie's voice trailed off as she searched for some way to describe the mental and emotional attack, but to no avail. "It wasn't until this morning that the storm began to fade away. She was distracted."

"By the funeral," said Zéolie. She took Angelie's hand in hers and explained the details to the fragile nun of the funeral events that kept Solène occupied. "Celeste'll recover, but that demon managed to terrorize half the French Quarter. There's just so much hate in her, yet she seems thoroughly amused by everything. Trying to shut her out has gotten harder. Sometimes it feels like my mind isn't my own anymore, and it's exhausting to keep her at bay. She's always there, lurking in the shadows even when she's not blatantly amusing herself at my expense. I'm not sure I have it in me to fight much longer."

The two friends sat in silence searching for the right words to console the other without success.

Angelie's eyes flitted to the door an instant before one of the sisters knocked softly. "Officer Saucier's here, mademoiselle."

"Thank you," Zéolie replied as she stood and smoothed her skirts. Turning to Angelie, she said, "I had her send word to Louis that you were better. Tell him I'll see him in the parlor, sister." Sister Mary Clare nodded and went to deliver the message.

Swinging her legs off the edge of the bed, Angelie rose. "I'm going with you."

In the parlor, Zéolie and Angelie filled Louis in on Solène's grip on the young nun's mind and the silent war Camille waged trying to keep Angelie safe. "There is one thing that I can't make sense of in all of this," Louis began as he paced the parlor floor.

"*One* thing?" Zéolie asked incredulously.

Louis blushed to the roots of his curls. "You're right, of course. None of it makes any logical sense, but this has to do with the cemetery. Why was that rose worth trying to kill Angelie over? And how did you know it would turn her rage on you?"

"That's two things," Angelie said with a smile. Louis blushed again. "At first, all I had was a feeling, like Camille gives me when she's trying to get through to me. I knew the rose was symbolic of something, and it was important to her, but I didn't know why. I certainly didn't know what would happen if I took it."

"That was a very brave thing you did," Zéolie said softly.

Angelie shifted uneasily in her chair. "No, it had nothing to do with bravery. I hardly gave it any thought at all. It was as if I had no choice but to do it. As if Camille was using me somehow."

"So, you don't know why taking the rose angered her so much?" Louis asked stopping his pacing. Shoving his hands in his pockets, he rocked on his heels in thought.

Angelie shook her head. "Not at the time. Since then, I have a better idea of why. It was laid there by Julien years ago when the tomb was sealed. It was his last gesture of love for Solène. As much as she's grown to hate him, she still needed him to love her."

Louis' brow knit in confusion. "How could you know that?"

Zéolie smiled at him. "Sounds like you've forgotten who you're talking to. Was that Camille, too?" she asked Angelie.

She nodded. "I wish I could explain to you how I know these things, Louis, but I can't. I don't understand it myself."

Louis paced to the window and looked out at the officers standing at their posts. "I know, and it's alright. My problem is how to put all of this into a police investigation. We all know there's something very strange happening here, but we still have to focus on the facts and evidence. Police officers aren't supposed to go rushing around New Orleans on a ghost hunt."

"Witch hunt," Angelie corrected bluntly.

"Either way, I can't put that in a report."

"So, what do we do now?" Zéolie began. "My mother, who is supposed to be dead, is a voice in my head trying to kill my friends after murdering a priest and my father, and the only one with any power to stop her is my long-dead witch grandmother who talks to a nun!" Zéolie took a deep breath and looked from Angelie to Louis expectantly. "There," she said after a pause. "Put that in your police report."

CHAPTER
NINE

Orange and pink washed across the sky as the sun hovered on the western horizon. Hoping a change of scenery would bring clarity or escape, the three made their way from the closeness of the parlor to the open courtyard. Cooling night air felt good on their faces as they wandered the garden in relative silence. No one wanted to talk about the disturbing events of the day anymore, but none could get their minds off them.

Endless lilting singsong and giddy laughter in her mind drove Zéolie to distraction. The song rose and fell, words changed from nonsense to bawdiness. Occasionally the singing would stop as she laughed at her own cleverness. It was better than the rage, Zéolie told herself. Anything was better than that. Solène was in a good mood.

Zéolie settled down on the sweeping branch of the live oak tree where she and Angelie sat days before. They were no closer to ending the chaos than they were then. So much happened since that only added to the confusion. Answers only led to more questions as the web of lies, rumors, and mystery spun more and more out of control.

Trying to shut out the madness of her mother and the chaos of her life, Zéolie leaned against the rough bark and closed her eyes.

Angelie paced around the garden running her hands along the tops of the day lily blooms that began to close with the sunset. She said little since Zéolie's outburst in the parlor and reverted to her reserved unemotional self. At the end of the row of drooping flowers, Angelie stopped her pacing and stood motionless for a moment. Zéolie and Louis had become used to the odd quirks of the nun, so this didn't draw notice from either of them. After a little while, Angelie said, "I have to go inside. There's something I need to do," then turned on her heel and strode out of the courtyard leaving Louis and Zéolie alone.

Zéolie stole a sidelong glance at Louis as he stood nearby examining a cricket more closely than anyone would. He shifted his weight from one foot to the other, then shoved his hands deep in his pockets. Zéolie closed her eyes and pretended not to notice as she tried to be innocently inconspicuous herself. After a moment, Louis broke the tension with a grin. "We've been in enough danger lately; do you think we should add the wrath of the mother superior if she finds us alone out here?" he teased.

Zéolie laughed and swung herself off the tree branch. "Probably not, but she's a very busy woman. I'm sure it'll be a little while before we're noticed." She saw the color rise in his cheeks and knew she was blushing, too. With a sparkle in her eye, she looped her arm through his and began to stroll the garden in silence again. Her chest fluttered as she settled her arm into the strong, but gentle crook of his.

Louis fell in step beside her, his heart pounding in his tightening chest. *She's just a victim in an investigation,* he lied to himself once more. As they walked the garden paths, the sun sank with deep purples and blues into the horizon. Fireflies danced among the tightly closed day lily blooms. A breeze picked up a strand of Zéolie's hair and draped it across her face. Her cheek rested on his arm as she brushed her hair out of her face. Louis stopped and looked down at Zéolie for a long moment. She smiled, and a shiver raced through him. Before he knew it, Louis slipped his arm around her waist, holding her close to him. The warmth of her radiated through him, and he felt her relax into his embrace as if she belonged there. A shrill whistle sounded in the distance breaking the spell of the moment, and he realized how he let himself get carried away by the night. The whistle signaled the shift change for the convent guards. At that instant, the reality of their situation came crashing back down on them.

Zéolie stepped back and lowered her eyes. "I should go."

Louis raised her hand to his lips and kissed the back of it. "You need to get some rest. Goodnight, Zéolie."

Impulsively, Zéolie rose to her tiptoes and kissed him gently on the corner of his mouth. "Goodnight, Louis," she whispered.

With that, she was gone, but his lips tingled in the place where hers had been a moment before. Turning and walking around to the front of the convent to make his way back to the station in the Ninth Ward, Louis was more determined than ever to end the nightmare churning around them.

Clouds skittered across the dark sky on the wind that gently swirled over the river and traipsed through the convent garden. With gentle breaths, it rattled the glass pane in the window of the convent cell. Zéolie lay in her bed in the tiny room that had been hers since she arrived. Even as stark as it was, she found peace in the close space. She needed peace so badly. Her mind darted relentlessly to everywhere but sleep. While most of her thoughts revolved around her father's death at her mother's hands and the confusion swirling around it all, she couldn't help but think of Louis. The smell of him as she tripped into his arms, the softness in his expression when she needed reassurance, the crinkling at the edges of his eyes when he was thinking through the bizarre facts, the warmth of the edge of his mouth on her lips. As much as she wanted to do it, she regretted that small kiss she gave Louis. Her feelings for him bubbled to the surface, but she pushed them back down and held them there, hoping to drown them before her mother realized what was happening. Sinister laughing in her head told her it was already too late. Louis, like everyone else she loved, was now in mortal danger.

Hours seemed to pass as Zéolie tried in vain to get some sleep. Tossing and turning in the tiny bed, her heart ached for her father more than ever. Every thought of him resulted in snarling comments from Solène. *He was a damn fool, Zéolie. Be glad you're rid of him! Julien was arrogant and weak.* Desperately, she tried to silence the voice, but it refused to relent.

Somewhere in the distance, as she fought the mental battle with her mother, she heard a soft tapping sound. It grew louder, and she pulled herself out of the depths of her own mind realizing there was someone at her door. "Zéolie!" Angelie whispered. "Are you awake?"

"It's alright, Angelie. Come in. You didn't wake me."

Angelie pushed open the door and set the candle she was carrying on the bedside table. "Get dressed. There's someone we need to see."

Zéolie was used to Angelie's strange ways but stood dumbstruck at the thought of going out in the dead of night. "Now?"

Angelie nodded, handing Zéolie her dress that was laid across the back of the small wooden chair in the corner. "Put this on. The mourning black will be just what you need. Hurry." The nun turned her back to give Zéolie some privacy as she changed into the dress. "Put your hair up," Angelie instructed, picking the hairpins up from the table. "You don't want it to get snagged."

"Snagged?" Nothing about that sounded good.

"You'll see."

Knowing full well she wasn't going to get more out of Angelie until the nun was ready to tell her, Zéolie obediently twisted her hair up at the nape of her neck and pinned it in place. She trusted the nun, but nerves still gathered in her chest making her breath come fast and shallow. Angelie placed a finger on her lips as she held the door open for Zéolie and the two made their way silently down the convent halls. With her heart pounding in her chest and the singsong in her ears darker and louder now, Zéolie pushed the maniac to the back of her mind and wondered how they would slip past the guards stationed around the perimeter. Even though they were there to protect her, not confine her, Zéolie knew the officers would not allow her to go anywhere without an escort. There was something telling her that wherever the nun was taking her, they needed to go alone. Angelie reached the main hall, but instead of going to the front doors, she turned toward a door that revealed another hallway entrance and motioned for Zéolie to follow.

Darkness consumed the passageway except for a glimmer of golden light at the far end. Underfoot, the wood was warped from neglect, not worn smooth like the common halls. Instinctively, Zéolie placed a hand on the wall to steady herself. She focused on the light when she could see it, but with Angelie leading the way, she was mostly dependent on the wall to guide her. Curiosity pushed questions to her lips she wouldn't dare to ask even in the seeming emptiness of the expanse of corridor. Periodically, fingers sliding along the plaster wall would bump across a door, but the shadow of the nun moved silently forward. Angelie appeared to be heading straight for the far end.

Light loomed brighter as they approached the opening and Zéolie saw that it was a single candle on a table that was their guide. To one side of the table was a dark flight of stairs, but these weren't the destination either. Angelie put a thin finger through the loop of the brass candleholder and led Zéolie down another shorter corridor that ended in a large wooden door. Pulling a thin iron key from her habit, Angelie slid it into the lock. Metal scraped on metal as the bolt slid free. Freshly oiled hinges eased the heavy door open as the two women stepped cautiously outside.

Sitting a safe distance from the main structure in case of fire was the detached servant kitchen. Moonlit smoke curled up from the chimney against the clear night sky. Comforting smells of simmering food and fire filled the air. Zéolie followed Angelie around the back of the kitchen and realized there were no guards on this far point of the property. Angelie saw Zéolie's gaze darting nervously around her. Pointing to the small kitchen building, she mouthed "Inside, eating," and laid her finger on her lips again. Noiselessly, the pair slipped through the shadows past the building and into the night.

Above, clouds tumbled across the sky taking most of what little moonlight there was with them. Ahead in the distance, Zéolie could make out the dark shape of a small carriage. The horse stood so motionless that Zéolie began to wonder if she was really seeing it at all. Angelie picked up her pace and made a low whistle. It was answered by a matching whistle from a figure standing at the horse's head holding the reins.

Zéolie didn't recognize the driver as one of the convent slaves, but Angelie nodded in recognition and got in. Whoever he was, the man was exactly who Angelie expected to be there. Once they were both settled and moving down the dirt road, Zéolie finally spoke. "Where are we going?"

Angelie stared at her a moment seeming to weigh her words before she spoke. "I need you to trust me."

Zéolie nodded but was uneasy about being led into the night without Louis and not knowing where they were going. Nothing about the past few days had been predictable and if her mother couldn't be held at bay by a funeral mass, nowhere was safe. At least the convent had an illusion of safety. Zéolie sighed and resigned herself to getting answers, even if it meant risking her life in the middle of the night on an insane errand with a cryptic nun.

She looked out through a small opening in the carriage curtain into the night. Something was different, and it made her more uneasy as she tried to figure out what it was. Fighting something she couldn't see was making her edgy and wary. Terror she could see coming was fearsome enough, but there was something deeply ominous about the unknown and unseen. When death lurked just out of sight, there was no time for letting her guard down. Every second of every day, she had to constantly brace for anything her mother may decide to do. Any mad and deadly possibility.

Inky blackness surrounded them as the thin sliver of moon slipped behind a cloud. The only sound was the pounding of her heart in her ears and the soft thuds of the horse's hooves on the dirt. Even the carriage must have been freshly oiled to not make a sound in the night. That was it. That's what was so eerily different. No other sound. As she listened to the quiet around her, she realized that even Solène had gone silent. This should have been a welcome relief, but instead, the sudden absence of the voice filled her with dread.

Where are you? What are you doing? Zéolie wondered. Nothing. No laugh, no mocking, no rage-filled tirade. The silence in her mind was deafening.

Angelie stared at a space a few feet in front of her. Only this time, it wasn't stunned catharsis She seemed to be listening to something. Was she hearing the nothingness, too?

They rode on through the night on pitted rural roads away from New Orleans to the wild outskirts until the carriage could take them no further. Bathed in intermittent moonlight as the clouds swept across the sky, the cypress trees rose like shadowy sentinels above the black swamp. Other than the rutted road, there was no sign of civilization anywhere.

"Why are we stopping?" Zéolie whispered to the driver as he handed her down from the carriage.

The whites of his eyes narrowed in his ebony face. "The horse can't go any further, ma'amselle. You go on foot from 'ere." His voice had only a hint of a Haitian lilt to it but was strangely free of the accent she was familiar with slaves in New Orleans having. He had a strong deep voice that almost rumbled as he spoke. "Angelie knows the way. Stay with her and do as she says."

"You're not coming with us?" Zéolie asked. Fear seized her. She didn't know this man, but she had enough sense to know that two women had no business being out in the swamps in the middle of the night alone.

He took her hand in his to steady her panicked trembling. His hand was strong and smooth, not rough from years of hard labor. This man was no slave, but who was he? "No, ma'amselle. I've got somethin' else I have to do." With that, he bowed and swung himself up onto the driver's seat and gave the reins a snap. The horse and carriage disappeared into the night leaving the two women standing at the edge of the Louisiana swamps.

"Who was that?" Zéolie asked.

"A friend," Angelie answered vaguely. Zéolie realized she was going to get no more explanation out of the nun who was gathering the hems of her skirt and tying it in knots on the sides. "Tie up your skirts. You don't want them tripping you." Zéolie glanced at the tangle of vegetation in front of them and followed Angelie's example knotting up the sides of her layered skirts a few inches above her ankles. Once their skirts were secured, Angelie led Zéolie into the swamp with only the instruction to not make a sound, no matter what.

AIR HUNG close and thick in the depths of the soggy woods. The ground seemed to undulate beneath their carefully placed steps. One misstep and they would find themselves mired in the marshes that laced through the spongy land and cypress knees. The pair inched along the pathless swamp that held mysteries centuries old and worlds away from everything Zéolie knew.

The thin crescent moon seemed to cast spells and shadows, glittering on the water and shrouding the unexpected. An egret languidly raised her head from nestled sleep and contemplated the trespassers. Deeming them unworthy of alarm, she tucked her shimmering white head back under her wing as the women moved slowly on.

The swamp was far from silent in the dead of night. Sounds seemed to come from everywhere and nowhere at once. Wind whispered in her ears as frogs croaked at the water's edge. A hiss of grasses as something skittered past made her blood run cold. Zéolie was trembling through to her core, unsure if it was out of fear of her surroundings, or the unknown in her errand.

A deep guttural tone brought her feet and her breathing to a halt. Eyes widened as she searched the darkness helplessly for the monster. Her breath rushed back to her in shallow gasps as her fear mounted. The deep unearthly growl came from just feet in front of her. Zéolie couldn't make out the reptile in the dark but could feel its eyes on her.

Angelie heard it, too. The nun was not afraid of the night or the swamp but knew the deadliness of a mother alligator. Her hand closed around her rosary as she took a slow, long breath. Zéolie clutched the crucifix at her neck with a cold shaking hand.

The throaty rumble began to retreat with a rustling of grasses as the mother monster backed away to her nest. It was several moments before either of the women moved. Angelie went first, taking Zéolie by the arm as they continued their slow arduous trek across the wilds.

Deep in the black heart of the swamp, a glimmer of golden light broke through the darkness. Zéolie squinted trying to separate the shadows from one another as Angelie urged her silently on. The pair inched forward, and a house began to take shape in the darkness ahead. Zéolie hoped it would be place of salvation, but it could just as easily be the mouth of hell.

She was so focused on the small sliver of light and the silhouette of the house that she lost her footing and sank into the mud. As she stumbled, a man's hand caught her elbow and another strong hand smothered the cry that escaped her lips. Zéolie whirled around and locked eyes with the same ebony face that had reassured her as she stepped out of the carriage at the edge of the swamp. In the sliver of moonlight, she saw him smile at her. "Shhh.

Careful, now. You're almost there," he whispered then went on leading the way.

"Where- Where did he come from?" Zéolie asked Angelie.

"Putting the horse up. We can't go that way. It's dangerous."

A chill raced through Zéolie as she thought of anything more treacherous than the path they took.

"She's waiting for us. Let's go," Angelie said with her usual abruptness and stepped around the confused Zéolie. With more confident steps as the ground became more solid, the nun led the way to the house in the shadows.

As they grew nearer to the cabin, candles began to appear in the windows. Light streamed out of the grime-covered panes to illuminate the landscape around the building. It seemed precariously balanced on the cypress stilts that kept it above the rising and falling swamp waters. Steps that led to the covered porch were warped and cracked at the bottom where years of being repeatedly submerged had taken its toll on them. Lichen grew in the splintered gaps Above, Spanish moss dripped off the edges of the covered porch. In one corner, the lace of a huge spider web glinted in the moonlight. Zéolie could hardly believe this was their destination. What could Angelie possibly hope to find here?

As they climbed the steps, the door creaked open and warm golden light spilled out onto the porch. In the doorway, with one hip slung out to the side and a hand resting lightly on her slender waist, stood a woman unlike any Zéolie had ever seen. Layers of skirts and scarves in rich colors seemed to hover around her, swirling as she moved to motion them inside. Her head was wrapped in a tignon of deep reds, oranges, and greens, and her skin was the color of fine caramel. Behind long black lashes, mossy green eyes glittered in the candlelight. Bracelets clinked softly on her wrists and rings glinted on her fingers. She was both stunning and strange.

"I've been waitin' for you, cherie," the woman said in a rich silken voice as she took Zéolie's hand in hers. "This night's been a long time comin'." There was a softness in the Haitian accent that reassured Zéolie a bit even if the woman herself seemed ethereal and exotic.

"I'm sorry, but I don't understand," Zéolie said softly.

Angelie spoke up. "This is Mama Nell. She's your...godmother, so to speak."

Zéolie looked at the strange vision before her and tried desperately to make sense of what was just said. "I don't—"

"—understan,'" Mama Nell finished. "I know. Come in an' I'll explain." She led them to a small circle of chairs in a corner of the house. As they walked through, Zéolie realized the cabin was a single room divided by furniture and shelves. Lining the walls were small boxes, bottles, and jars. It was difficult to tell what was inside them all. There were few labels and the ones that did exist were aged and illegible. A long workbench was on one side of the room with more jars and other odd things scattered on top. Herbs, small sacks, and nets hung from the rafters stretched across the room below the high vaulted ceiling designed to let the heat rise well above the living space. The whole place was tidy but covered in layers of dust in varying thicknesses. An earthy mustiness mingled with the fragrances of herbs Zéolie couldn't identify. Then, she noticed something she didn't expect to find in a place like this. Books. Shelves of them. Some were leather-bound while others appeared to have been hand sewn to bind them. All of them were old and well-worn.

"I s'pose I should start from the beginnin'," Mama Nell said as she draped herself on one of the armchairs. It was almost as if she was liquid. Every motion seemed to flow from the last to the next. There was a mysterious elegance about her that wasn't cold and pretentious like the socialite airs Zéolie was used to.

The black man from earlier brought a tray of coffee in and set it on a small table next to Mama Nell. "Thank you, Vernand." Zéolie saw him give Mama Nell a wink as he stepped back into the shadows until needed again. *A bit more than a servant,* Zéolie thought. With movements that would shame a dancer, Mama Nell poured coffee for her guests, completely at ease in her house in the middle of the terrifying swamp.

"Thank you," said Zéolie taking the cup offered to her. She inhaled the rich aroma of the black coffee and could smell the touch of chicory in it. Slowly, she sipped it and let the warmth and comfort of the drink still her shaking hands.

"Now, child, lemme explain all this to you," Mama Nell began. She sat back in her chair, draped one of her long legs over the other one, and rested her cup on her knee. "Angelie says you know about Camille an' Solène an' who they are to you." Mama Nell looked at Angelie who nodded. "But it seems the time's come for me to tell you what the mother superior didn't. Camille didn't come to New Orleans by accident when she fled France. What they said 'bout her was true. She was a witch an' a damned good one, but she wasn't anyone to fear," Mama Nell added as Zéolie's eyes widened. "Oh, she could've been, but she didn't have a black spot on her heart."

"Did you know my grandmother?" Zéolie asked.

Mama Nell shook her head. "I didn't have the pleasure. My mama knew her an' I heard all the stories growin' up."

"But I thought Camille died of an illness not long after she arrived here." Zéolie's head swam with trying to keep the facts and half-truths straight. Now, there was even more to decipher.

"She did, cherie, but she an' my mama went way back. Camille's father owned a sugar plantation in Haiti an' my mama was a young slave there. When Camille was almost eighteen, her papa brought her to the plantation to learn about the place since it'd be hers one day. She took more interest in the Voodoo ceremonies than the work of the plantation, an' soon she an' my mama were fast friends. It was 'bout that time, too, that strange things started to happen." Mama Nell paused and took a slow sip of her coffee letting the information sink in to Zéolie's mind.

"What things were happening?" Zéolie asked after a moment. As bizarre as it seemed, she was finding herself caught up in the odd woman's story.

"Camille had an uncanny ability with fortune cards. She learned 'em quickly an' was almost never wrong. Unfortunately, what she saw in the cards in readin's for others happened to her instead." As Mama Nell spoke those words, Zéolie's face went white as her thoughts flashed to the Hanged Man reading for Lisette and the death of her father. The Hanged Man. Those cards were intended as a warning for her, not Lisette. Mama Nell smiled and nodded. "I see you've had the same thing happen to you, cherie. If you don' pay attention to the universe, it has a way of makin' you notice what it wants you to. Seems you an' your granmother have more in common than you thought," Mama Nell said with a wink. "Angelie said your gifts were stronger than you realized. Maybe it's time you start payin' attention."

"But she fights her gifts," Angelie added. "If she would only let go and use them, she could do so much more."

"I don't know what you're talking about, Angelie. I don't have gifts. All I have is an insane woman's voice in my head! At least...I did. She's..."

"Gone?" Mama Nell asked. Zéolie nodded. "Don't count on it. She might be distracted by somethin', but she won't be gone for long!" All Zéolie could think about was the menacing laugh in her head any time her thoughts drifted to Louis. The pit of her stomach tightened in dread.

Mama Nell continued, "You've got the same gifts my mama saw in Camille. My grandmother was a priestess on the plantation an' took Camille under 'er wing. Night after night, my mama'd sneak Camille out of the plantation house through the slave corridors an' down to the cabins. Inside those walls, they conjured all kinds of things from dancing white mists to spirit possessions. Camille grew stronger an' more controlled every night. Mama worked tirelessly to teach Camille everythin' she could. She learned candle magic, powder spells, Haitian Voodoo rituals, an' anythin' else Mama could teach her under the cover of night. Every year when it was time to do the business of the harvest, Camille'd come with her papa and her trainin' would pick up where they left off. That's how it was, right up until the slaves revolted an' it all came crashin' down. My grandmother an' mama found passage to New Orleans by callin' in some favors owed to 'er, an' they settled here as free women." The priestess paused again. She seemed to know how difficult all of this was for Zéolie to take in and was trying to give the girl time to absorb it in small doses. Zéolie was familiar with stories of the Haitian Revolution. Many of the slaves settled in New Orleans as free people of color, gens de couleur libre. They were part of the very fabric of the city. She had no idea how much the gens de couleur were a part of her fabric, too.

"Did they ever see each other again?" Zéolie asked.

Mama Nell shook her head and lowered her green eyes. "Sadly, no. My mama learned to write a little an' would sneak letters to Camille an' she'd send my mama spells she learned in France. That European witchcraft was powerful stuff an' Camille was gaining immense strength. The two of 'em had to be real careful because they were afraid if Camille's papa found out where his slaves had gone he'd try to take 'em back. When your grandmother faced exile in France, she wrote to my mama tellin' her she was comin' to New Orleans. By this time, her skills were stronger'n any my mama could imagine an' she was anxious to see her old friend. She never would. Camille died before they got the chance but sent word to my mama about Solène an' asked her to watch over the child."

"How would she do that if Solène was in the convent?" Angelie asked.

"Mama couldn't do it herself, but she had connections among the slaves there. But she found another way to keep her promise to Camille. It got its start a few years before your grandmother's exile. A handsome young man came here to see my mama one night. He had a business partner he didn't trust an' came to her to seek answers in the cards. Mama's advice saved his business an' he started comin' to see her about everythin'. Soon, the visits became less about the cards an' more about her. The young man had fallen for her an' they began a love affair that'd last until the day he died."

"Who was he?"

Mama Nell toyed with the end of one of her many scarves a moment before lifting her eyes to meet Zéolie's. "That young man was Armand Cheval."

Zéolie's head swam. Her *grandfather*? "Are you..."

"...your aunt? Yes," Mama Nell answered slowly. "Your father was my half-brother. It was some careful manipulation by my mama that your parents married. She knew from Camille that Solène had a large inheritance an' that fact'd make her an acceptable choice for the young Cheval heir. An' it'd get the girl closer to her when she turned twenty-one an' the powers she no doubt inherited would need trainin'. It certainly didn't hurt that Julien was as handsome as his father an' Solène fell in love with him instantly."

"He loved her, too. All he ever told me of her was how beautiful and loving she was," Zéolie sighed setting her empty coffee cup on the table between a painted stone and a candle stump. "I can't believe the woman he loved so much is the maniac in my head."

"There was a long time that what he told you of 'er was true. He loved that girl unconditionally an' she loved him. Solène refused to hide what she really was from 'im an' he allowed her to learn to harness her power- 'long as she kept it hidden from everyone else. He was afraid she'd face the same ridicule her mother did an' wanted to shield her from that as much as he could. Julien would've moved heaven an' earth for Solène."

"Something must've happened, though. He told me she died in childbirth, but it was all a lie. Why would he do that? Where's she been all this time?"

Mama Nell and Angelie exchanged glances. Those very questions were why Angelie brought Zéolie through the swamp. "I wish I could tell you where she's been, but the woman your father loved *did* die, in a sense," Mama Nell answered. "She'd inherited Camille's powers, but that wasn't all. Solène also inherited the madness of 'er father.

Her husband's madness was the reason for Camille's exile. For years, her secret'd been safe with 'im an' they lived happily in France. After Solène was born, madness took over 'im. He told stories of dark sordid nights of witchcraft and debauchery that were far from anythin' Camille would've done. It was his madness that drove the stories, but there was enough truth in what he said 'bout his wife to raise suspicion. 'Fore long, she found herself runnin' for her life to New Orleans."

"What happened to my grandfather?"

"He was put in a sanitarium to 'cure' his bewitchment that was supposedly put on 'im by his wife. One night he was found dead. Hung himself by tyin' his bedsheets aroun' his neck and bedpost, then jumpin' out 'is window."

Zéolie gasped. "That's horrible!"

Mama Nell nodded. "It was sad, but livin' with his madness must've been torture." She drifted in thought for a moment before continuing. "After a few years, Solène started actin' real strange, bein' overjoyed one minute, then collapsin' into great heavin' sobs the next. She'd fly into a jealous rage anytime Julien spoke to one of the servant women—old or young, didn't matter to her. Then, she'd be as tender as a kitten to 'im. Still, he loved her an' did all he could to soothe her.

"When she told 'im she was expectin' their child, he was overjoyed. Julien hoped the baby'd bring her the peace she seemed at a loss for. Sadly, over time, things only got worse. The slaves of the house talked 'bout strange rituals with the child, and the mother's mutterin's in the baby's ears. In New Orleans, things like that weren't as feared like they were other places, but one night changed all that."

"What happened?" Zéolie's voice was barely over a whisper.

Mama Nell took a deep breath and rose from the chair. She moved to the window and gazed out into the blackness. Silence filled the room broken only by the tiny scratchings of a mouse scuttling across the floor. The priestess stood motionless and statuesque with her back to Zéolie as she spoke. "Your father'd taken to checkin' on you an' your mother durin' the night an' was goin' to your room when he heard singin'. It was your mother down in the courtyard. He opened your door to look in on you, but your crib was empty. Julien raced down to the courtyard an' saw the glint of steel in the moonlight as Solène raised a dagger above his sleepin' child on the ground in front of her." Graceful shoulders bent as a sob caught in her throat. Taking a slow breath, Mama Nell continued, "He—he dove at her as the knife came down at you an' threw Solène to the ground. Her head hit the bricks knockin' her unconscious. She was alive, but badly hurt. No one, not even the woman he loved, was gonna hurt his precious baby girl."

Tears streamed down Zéolie's face as her aunt talked through her own tears. "Julien knew he had to get Solène away from you or she'd try it again but couldn't bring himself to kill her. The only thing he could think to do was fake her death, so no one would ask questions 'bout where she'd gone or what she'd done. Your father wrapped her unconscious body in bedsheets an' then a carriage took Solène away into the night. Julien set the kitchen ablaze an'....an' killed one of the slave girls." Mama Nell paused for a moment, overcome by the emotional pain. When she finally collected herself, she went on, "He threw the girl's corpse into the kitchen fire an' let it burn enough to be unrecognizable before he began battlin' the blaze so there'd be a body in the wreckage for neighbors to see when they came to help. By the time the neighborhood got the fire under control, there was nothin' left of the body to bury." The elegance and liquid grace of Mama Nell from earlier in the evening was a stark contrast to the statue at the window. Her knuckles whitened as she gripped the back of the chair trying to steady herself.

Zéolie shook her head to get rid of the image of her father murdering one of his slaves. Tears poured unchecked down her face as she pictured him throwing the girl's body into the flames to fake the death of the woman he loved even in her madness. After a moment, she was able to ask, "Other people knew what supposedly happened to my mother. Why wasn't that the story he told me? Why did no one else tell me that?"

"Your father thought the story of Solène burnin' to death was too much for a child to hear, so he asked anyone who might say anythin' to you to tell you she died in childbirth. Your father bein' respected for the man he was, they swore on their lives they'd keep that secret."

"Where did they take Solène?"

The priestess slowly turned to face her. "To my mother's cabin. Here."

Angelie's face went white. "But that means she knows where this is! She could find us!"

"Shush, now, Angelie," Mama Nell said. "She can find Zéolie anywhere we try to hide 'er. They're connected by blood. There's no changin' that."

"What happened after they brought her here?" Zéolie asked.

"My mama took care of 'er best she could while keepin' her sedated. She knew you and Julien weren't safe 'long as Solène was alive but didn't want the blood of the witch's death on 'er hands. So, she gathered some of the priests and priestesses of the old faith to help her make sure Solène wouldn't be able to hurt you again. The rituals lasted all night, but by the time they were done, there was enough protection 'round you and your father to keep you safe 'til you were old enough to use your gifts to defend yourself."

"Twenty-one. Until I turned twenty-one."

Mama Nell nodded.

Zéolie had more answers now, but, like always, even more questions. Throbbing pain settled in her temples as she tried to absorb the new information and connect it to what she'd learned from the mother superior. The more she learned about her mother, the more dangerous Solène became. Mama Nell told her all she knew but knowing the events of the past wasn't enough to defend herself against her mother. If she was going to do be able to defeat the force that was stalking her, she needed help. Mama Nell agreed with Angelie that she needed Camille.

"I just don't understand how Camille can help me if I can't talk to her. She only talks to Angelie."

Mama Nell nodded. "Now she does. Angelie's right, though. Once you open up an' let yourself go, you'll be able to connect with 'er, too. You're bound to 'er by blood, just like Solène. Angelie's bound to 'er in a different way. You need to open up your blood bonds an' embrace what Camille's given you. Then, you can begin to defend yourself with 'er help. Solène doesn't want to hurt you because you're far too valuable to 'er. If she could corrupt you, the two of you'd be a force to be reckoned with."

"But I would never—" Zéolie began.

"I know that, Zéolie. An' somewhere deep down Solène must know it, too, or she wouldn't be so hell bent on destroyin' everyone who knew what she was up to."

"Father Antoine knew?" Angelie asked.

Mama Nell nodded. "Yes, he did. I said Mama got the priests and priestesses of the old faith, remember? Well, he was at that ritual, too. Father Antoine hoped that where the old faith failed, the Catholic faith would succeed. He knew no matter how old you were, she couldn't take you by force. You'd have to go to 'er willin'ly. He died for that knowledge."

Zéolie stared at Mama Nell for a moment. "But you have that knowledge, too. You aren't safe, either, are you?"

"None of us are, cherie. None of us are."

CHAPTER

TEN

As the darkest hours of the night set in over the Louisiana swamp, Zéolie, Angelie and Vernand prepared to set out for the city. Mama Nell began her own preparations before letting them venture out into the night. Lighting a white votive candle, she placed it in front of a small black mirror and took a deep breath. "There's much to do if I'm gonna try to keep you safe on the journey home. You keep your wits about you, now. I'll do what I can, but can't say if it'll be powerful enough to combat anythin' Solène could do."

As the trio stepped out of the cottage, lightning flashed in the distance. For an instant in the white light, the swamp was beautiful. Spanish moss draped over the cypress branches swaying in the gathering wind like a lace curtain in an open window. Lightning glittered across the black swamp water and a deep rumble of thunder rolled over the trees around her. As the flashes flickered and died, darkness closed in once again, shrouding the way home. Step by tentative step, they made their way towards the hidden marsh path. Morning would come soon, but the gathering clouds made the dark of the wee hours more oppressive. Minutes seemed like hours in the tension of the treacherous swamp. Unseen and unknown dangers lurked in every shadow. Zéolie tried to follow Angelie's careful steps but floundered as she lost sight of the nun in the inky depths. Vernand was ahead of them somewhere in the distance, but even in the blinding flashes of lightning, he couldn't be seen.

The approaching storm began to illuminate the landscape in frantic bursts. As Zéolie sank ankle-deep into the sucking mud, she saw Angelie reach up and push a low-hanging vine out of the way, but it didn't move aside. Instead, it slid around her arm and up to her shoulder. Angelie flailed in blind panic as it twisted tighter and tighter winding around her neck. Zéolie wrenched her foot free of the mire in a mad scramble to get to Angelie but sank deeper with her next step the more she struggled. There was a flash of white as the snake opened its mouth and sank its fangs into Angelie's throat. Pulling and clawing at the beast, Angelie fought hard but couldn't free herself. As she struggled, the water moccasin coiled tighter pumping venom into her veins. Her face, that had been pale in the lightning, turned crimson, then deep purple. A sickening gurgle was the only sound she made as Angelie turned wild frightened eyes on her friend.

"*No!*" Zéolie shrieked. "*Vernand!*" Her heart pounded, and breath came in frantic shallow gasps as she pushed against the bog. As Angelie slid to the ground, Vernand leaped out of the darkness and caught her. Finally finding stable footing, Zéolie lunged toward where Angelie collapsed, but he put up a hand to stop her coming any closer to the snake that was now loosening its grip. As it released, Vernand's quick hand caught the tail of the cottonmouth and whipped it into a tree trunk, smashing its skull. He started trying to suck out the venom from Angelie's wound, but the effort was useless. Vernand looked up at Zéolie with wide pained eyes. Panting with exhaustion and adrenaline, he sank to his hands and knees.

Emotions boiled just under Zéolie's skin as she struggled to keep control of the energy coursing through her body. Fear, anger, and grief surged out of her in a shockwave of electricity. Lightning burst from the palms of her hands striking the mighty cypress behind Angelie and Vernand, igniting it in a shower of sparks. Solène's wild maniacal laughter rang through the swamp. *"Shut up, you damned witch!"* Zéolie roared.

Flames danced along the treetops reflected in the black water of the deep swamp casting a hideous glare on the gruesome scene. Angelie clutched her rosary, brought the crucifix to her lips, then her arm fell limp by her side. Zéolie collapsed to the ground, tears glittering on her eyelashes in the firelight. Smoke swirled as the storm began to build, choking her as she tried to catch her breath. Sinking to her hands and knees in the mud, Zéolie sobbed as Angelie's body grew still and her eyes rolled up sightlessly toward the heavens.

Solène shrieked with laughter. "Where's your God *now*, Sister Angelie?" she cackled. "Give my regards to Father Antoine! I warned the little wench, but did she listen? *No!*"

Zéolie couldn't stand it anymore. Rising to her feet, she cried into the darkness, "Show yourself, you demon woman! It's *me* you want!"

The wild laughter turned into a syrupy-sweet voice. "Dear, sweet child! You know I love you more than anything. You are *mine*."

"I don't want your love!" Zéolie spat. "You've taken the things I love!"

"Not everything, mon petit chou!" Solène cooed. "Not everything."

Louis! thought Zéolie.

"That's right, my precious one. He lives... for now." Her mother's triumph at Angelie's death turned into a vicious laugh at the mention of the young officer.

Rage and fear surged inside of Zéolie as white-hot electricity raced down her arms to the palms of her hands. Throwing her head back, she released the energy and pain in a beastly scream. A bolt of lightning struck the water behind her and the jolt sent Vernand flying backwards. Angelie's limp body tumbled forward, her legs sinking into the black water. Zéolie kept her feet planted and seemed to be harnessing the energy from the bolt. Metal hairpins sparked and flew out of her hair, long dark strands standing on end around her pale face. Her dress whipped around her legs in the wind from the gathering storm, but Zéolie seemed to be in a trance holding her hands to the sky as if she could bring the very stars down from the heavens. Trembling, she pulled her hands to her chest, then threw the gathered energy as hard as she could at Angelie's limp body. Another shock of lightning broke overhead and the thunder drowned out Solène's taunting for an instant. Angelie's body shook violently but lay lifeless in the mud.

Vernand watched helplessly as Zéolie sank to her knees. Defeated, exhausted, and unconscious.

Darkness surrounded Zéolie's mind, total and haunting. Voices echoed in the blackness of the nothing surrounding her. Somewhere in the darkness, people were talking to her and about her, but what were they saying? She tried to open her eyes, to speak, to move, but her best efforts were futile and exhausting. Further away, deep in the recesses, a low laugh floated on an undulating wave of languid satisfaction. Relaxed. Pleased with herself. Even the echoes of laughter and voices faded as Zéolie slipped back into a troubled unconsciousness.

New sounds in the dark emptiness. Chanting, singing. Strange smells, earthy and warm. A hand was placed lightly across her forehead. Desperately wanting to see who it was, her mind begged her eyelids to open, but nothing happened. Something cool was poured into her mouth. Bitter. Her throat revolted and tried to spit it out but couldn't. Vile liquid slid down her throat, warming as it went. More chanting. More voices echoed. More empty blackness.

"Zéolie? Can you hear me?" a voice called. It was so far away she wasn't even sure she really heard it. Summoning all her strength, Zéolie managed a nod. It was the slightest movement, almost imperceptible, but it worked. "She's awake," the woman's voice said to someone nearby. She knew the voice, but who was it?

"Can she open her eyes? Does she know we're here?" another voice asked. Deeper than the first. A man's voice. Soft and worried. That voice was familiar, too.

"Give 'er some time. She's been through a lot," the first voice answered. A soft hand stroked her forehead. More earthy smells.

A stronger hand took hers. A man's hand. Zéolie struggled to open her eyes. At first all she managed was a flicker of lashes. *Damn it!* She cursed through the haze of her thoughts. Mentally tugging at her eyelids, she managed to force them slowly open. As she did, the room around her began to emerge from the darkness. At first, only a dimly lit swirl of color. Shadows collided with one another. Dull color faded into other dull colors. Zéolie blinked hard trying to bring things into focus, but the shimmering room wouldn't cooperate. A shadow moved across her face as the woman's soft hand passed over her eyes. Something cool was placed over them and the darkness returned. "Not yet, child," the woman said. "Sleep." With that, Zéolie slipped back into oblivion.

The next moment of consciousness was less surreal. There was a hollowness to the sounds around her, but not like the emptiness before. It was as if the space she was in was large and open compared to the last time she tried to come out of the abyss of sleep. This new place lacked the earthiness and warmth from the first time she tried to open her eyes. New smells. Ones she knew. Smells of wax candles and polished wood. Zéolie took a deep breath and tried again to open her eyes. Her lids fluttered and drew the attention of someone in the room. "She's coming around. Go wake the mother superior." Zéolie didn't know that voice, but it was soft and gentle. Opening her eyes, things began to slide into focus for the first time. She was in a place she didn't recognize, but it seemed familiar somehow. A candle glowing next to her on a small table pierced the darkness of the space with warm dancing light. Zéolie tried to ask where she was, but her voice wouldn't come. She tried to focus on the dark figure leaning over her, but all she saw was a shadow of the kind woman. "Shh, mademoiselle. Don't try to talk just yet. Let the sleep go first. There'll be plenty of time for talking later."

Zéolie relaxed her tense shoulders and sank back into the pillow, closing her heavy eyes. The warm earthy smells were gone. She'd liked those. This place smelled more like a hospital. Slowly, events from before began to drip into her mind through a sieve of muddled chaos. Little glimpses of things at first, then a trickle of memories. Mama Nell's house. Her aunt. A storm. The white mouth of a snake. "Angelie!" she cried out as her eyes flew open wide. Her raspy voice startled her. Frantically, she tried to sit up, but the woman urged her to lay back with a gentle pressure on her shoulder. Zéolie found she didn't have the strength to resist. Laying back on the pillow closing her eyes again, tears began to stream down the sides of her face. They ran into her hair and ears, but she didn't care. Zéolie let them flow silently as she spent what strength she had to mourn her friend and to mourn her own inability to save her.

A rustle of fabric at her bedside broke the trance of grief. "Zéolie, can you hear me?" a gentle older voice asked. Zéolie nodded. "Good. You're in the infirmary here at the convent. Sister Marie Lamonte says you've been a good patient."

Zéolie squinted her eyes and brought the figure on the edge of her bed into focus. Mother Micheaux. "Mother, I'm so sorry," Zéolie said through her tears.

The mother superior lowered her eyes. "I know, cherie, but you did all you could for her." Mother Micheaux sat on the edge of the bed and wiped a tear from Zéolie's cheek with a thin aging finger.

"It wasn't enough," Zéolie whispered struggling to get the words out.

Tears welled up in Mother Micheaux's eyes as she looked down at the young woman who had suffered so much loss. "Precious child, there was nothing more you could've done. She'll always be with you. Just like your father." The older woman took Zéolie's hand and folded it into both of hers. A tear broke through the barricade of fortitude and stole down her pale wrinkled cheek. "Right now, you need to concentrate on getting your strength back. You've got work to do."

Zéolie was having a difficult time making sense of much of anything. She knew the words but meaning escaped her grasp. "Work to do?" she asked. Her voice was a raspy whisper.

Mother Micheaux nodded as she rose from the edge of the bed. "Mama Nell will explain. Once you're stronger, the priestess can help you more than I can." With that, she placed her hand on Zéolie's forehead in blessing and quietly left the infirmary.

Zéolie laid there staring at the ceiling trying to piece together what her life had become, desperately wishing Angelie was with her to explain things. Somehow, having the quiet nun as a bridge between the earthly and the supernatural made things seem less insane. Now, she had the mother superior of the Ursuline nuns telling her she had work to do with her mulatto Voodoo priestess aunt she just met. Slipping back into the blackness of dreamless sleep, she said a silent prayer that this waking nightmare would end.

CHAPTER
ELEVEN

Dust danced like fairies in the sunbeams streaming through the parlor windows, stirred up by Louis' relentless pacing. One hand was shoved deep in his pocket as the other ran nervously through sandy curls. The ticking of the tiny brass clock seemed unnecessarily loud in the quiet of the convent.

Mother Micheaux sent him news that Zéolie regained consciousness during the night and he was anxious to find out more. His investigation of the murders was going nowhere with the normal police procedures and he knew the only way to get to the bottom of this was through Zéolie. But there was more than that, too. So much more.

He had been in a panic when he got news that she and Angelie were missing from the convent. Louis' first thought had, of course, been that Solène finally got what she wanted. Then, there was the strange man that arrived at the precinct in the night. The dark, well-spoken man answered few questions, but put Louis at ease even in the mysteriousness of his message: "Zéolie needs you. Mama Nell asked me to bring you to her." At once Louis felt relief that Zéolie was alive, but the fact that the Voodoo priestess had her sent a chill through him. Louis was an officer of the law. He shouldn't feel waves of fear about an old superstitious faith, but his own faith in logic had been shaken to its core by recent events. Supernatural things seemed as real and plausible as anything worldly at this point.

Once he made it to the cabin in the swamp and saw Zéolie lying there pale and lifeless, his heart ached and tears he made no effort to stop streamed down his face. Zéolie was breathing, but barely. Her clothes were singed, and her hair had lost its glossy luster. Mama Nell had bound much of it back in a long braid that lay next to the specter of the young woman who seemed so strong the evening before. Louis watched as Mama Nell and Vernand made poultices for the burned places on her arms, brewed potions of crushed herbs, and drained them down the girl's mouth, gently cradling her head to keep her from choking, and chanted murmured things he didn't understand. Around her body charms and stones were placed. On her heart was large black obsidian stone as big as the organ it rested over. Even in the warmth of the colored candles surrounding her, Zéolie still seemed almost ashen in complexion.

Louis stayed at her bedside and prayed he wouldn't lose her until Mama Nell assured him she was recovering enough to be taken to the convent infirmary. Most of the time, he sat on the floor by her bed watching the priestess work. He'd drift into fitful sleep holding Zéolie's hand until Mama Nell insisted he lay down and get some decent rest. She scolded him about being no use to Zéolie in his exhausted condition if she were to need him.

In the days and nights he spent there, the priestess told him little of what happened to Zéolie and refused to speak of Angelie at all. Once Mama Nell had done all she could for Zéolie with spells and charms to get her past the worst of the magical onslaught, Zéolie was moved to the convent infirmary to be treated by the nuns for her injuries. Louis reluctantly returned to the Ninth Ward precinct to await news. There were so many questions in need of answers, but Louis knew he couldn't ask Zéolie about them until she was stronger.

All he wanted in this moment was to see her open her eyes and know who he was.

It seemed like an eternity before Mother Micheaux came to get him from the parlor. "She can barely speak yet, but she seems to be more aware of where she is. She's out of danger," she paused, "from this, anyway." Louis instinctively crossed himself and breathed a deep sigh of relief then followed the mother superior down the long corridor.

Zéolie smiled up at Louis from her cot in the infirmary. It seemed like ages since their last moment in the courtyard. So much had happened...so much pain...but she didn't want to think about that now. She just wanted to drink in the sight of him standing there pushing curls out of his face and smiling down at her.

Mother Micheaux put her kind hand on Zéolie's. "I need to talk to Sister Mary Joseph for a moment, cherie." She stepped to the other side of the room to speak with the nurse on some pretense to give the two young people a moment to talk.

Tears once more welled up in Louis' eyes as he took in the pale figure of the woman who held his heart lying there drawn and weak. He practiced something official and polite to say all the way down the corridor following the mother superior's flowing robes to the infirmary. Now, he had no idea what that was. "Zéolie, you look— you look beautiful," was all he could say as he sat on the edge of the bed.

Zéolie managed a small laugh. "I hear hospitals have that effect on people," she teased in forced raspy words.

Louis dropped his eyes to the floor and blushed. "I'm- I'm sorry," he murmured. "I didn't mean—I shouldn't have—I'm sorry."

Zéolie put out her hand to him. Louis took it in his and she felt the warmth and strength she'd felt in the oblivion before and knew he'd been by her side. "Thank you, Louis," was all she said though there was more. So much more.

He held her hand a moment or two longer than the mother superior would have thought proper, but he didn't care. She was awake and smiling at him. That was all he wanted in the world.

Zéolie let Louis' strength pour into her. This moment couldn't last long, she knew, and she let herself sink into it. His eyes scanned her face and looked at her with a kindness that bore a striking resemblance to love. Zéolie couldn't let herself think that. It was dangerous, no matter how badly she wanted it to be true. The instant the emotion came over her, Solène's low laugh became more menacing. Louis was in very real danger as long as he was involved, but Zéolie knew he would never separate himself from her case just to save himself.

Mother Micheaux made her way back to Zéolie's bedside and Louis jumped up, letting her hand go like a little boy caught stealing sweets. The mother superior smiled at him but said nothing about it. Instead, she said to Zéolie, "Sister Mary Joseph wants you to stay and rest a little longer, and to eat something. If you're able to eat and get some strength back, she'll release you soon."

"Thank you, Mother," Zéolie answered. With a quick glance at Louis, she added, "I'm feeling better already." Louis blushed to the roots of his dark sandy curls, hoping desperately that no one noticed. Mother Micheaux placed her hand on Zéolie's forehead in blessing and stepped towards the infirmary door, pausing to wait for Louis.

For a moment, it seemed as though his feet were rooted to the spot. He didn't want to leave her, yet he knew propriety said he should. Zéolie held her hand out to him again. Taking it in his, Louis' lips brushed the back of her hand, then he slowly turned it over and softly kissed her wrist. He could almost feel her pulse quicken beneath his lips. Maybe it was his pulse; he couldn't say for sure and he didn't care. He loved her. He was sure of that.

∾

THE HOUSE on Dauphine was silent and still. A faded black wreath and heavily curtained windows stood as somber reminders of harrowing events that were now even wilder in the French Quarter rumors. Stories in New Orleans had a way of taking on a life of their own. They grew and spread like wildfire through the closeness of the city. Details would be added by those who 'knew these things,' others would swear they saw the dead with their own eyes when they were known to have been out of the city at the time, but no one would question these far-fetched additions to an already sensational tale. It would continue to burn through the hushed conversations of the matrons at parties and swirl through the cigar smoke of the gentlemen's parlors. Only the house, and a few people, knew that the truth was by far stranger than the fictions surrounding it, but the house stood deathly quiet.

In the distance, a voice called a greeting to someone on one of the wrought iron galleries down the block and lumbering carriages rattled past but Zéolie heard none of it. She stood as silent and motionless as the house she was staring at while the officers checked for any danger. Her home looked familiar and unfamiliar at the same time. Curtained windows looking out at her seemed sad somehow, as if the house knew how hard it was for her to be back at the scene of so much heartbreak. As if the house felt the pain of loss with her. Gone were the evenings full of laughter and friends playing cards while gossiping about fashion and love. Gone were the mornings of simple breakfasts in the courtyard and the comforting smells of dinner simmering in the kitchen. Gone were the quiet conversations of father and daughter in the cozy parlor on a rainy afternoon. All that remained of life in the house was sadness, pain, and lies.

Zéolie stood outside and watched as passers-by took a wide berth of the house that was so precious to her. To others it was a place of fear and ghost stories that entrenched themselves in the superstitions of the neighborhood. Some crossed themselves before and after passing by. Some stared at it as if they hoped they might see one of the specters said to roam the halls, while others refused to raise their eyes in fear of what they might see. A tear trickled down her cheek as she thought of the place she always adored becoming home to yet another New Orleans horror story.

Zéolie was brought out of her reverie when the front door opened, and Louis stepped out on to the front steps. He nodded at the officer who had been standing with Zéolie who nodded back then hurried back down the street mumbling something about another assignment. It was just as well he was gone. The poor man was a nervous wreck, pacing aimlessly and picking at his fingernails. He had jumped and twitched at every sound the entire time he was supposed to have been protecting her. Louis' presence was far more reassuring.

"Is everything alright?" Zéolie asked him, slipping her arm through the crook of his as he walked her up the steps.

Louis nodded. "It's all clear. You sure you want to do this?"

She took a deep breath and looked up at the second-floor windows. Sunlight glinted off the wavy glass and cast shadows from the ironwork onto the balcony wall. It seemed so normal, so lovely, this house of horror. "I'm sure," she answered trying to convince herself as much as Louis.

"We could wait outside for her instead if you want. We could even leave word for her to meet us somewhere else," Louis offered. "If this is too much for you..."

"No, Mama Nell was clear in her instructions. She said it was important that we work here." With another breath, she steeled her resolve to do what she needed to do, even if it meant risking another episode with her mother who had settled into a ridiculous sing-song again.

Louis nodded and pushed open the heavy front door. With one more cautious look inside, he held it for Zéolie. Crossing the threshold, she felt a tremor in her feet as though the house was startled she was there. Rooms were covered in a light layer of dust and smelled musty. Zéolie couldn't remember a time the house had been sealed up like this before. She and her father traveled often, but there were always servants at the house to tend to things in their absence. It seemed odd for the house she loved to smell like the inside of an old trunk.

"The house misses Delia. She would never approve of the dust," Zéolie said running a finger over the bottom of a picture frame.

"Delia loves you, but I'm not sure you'd ever get her back in this place," Louis answered. "She's still pretty shaken up."

Zéolie nodded. She didn't want to think about Delia, about what she had heard about her faithful caregiver.

Madame Marchon wrote to Delia's family offering any help she may need, and the response had been heartbreaking. The gentle woman who had taken care of Zéolie's family her whole life was completely dependent on others. She wouldn't speak and rarely slept. When she did sleep, nightmares would torture her. Often, Delia was found wandering the halls in her nightdress crying, but always without a sound. Doctors had been called to help her, but all they could do was sedate her so she could sleep. "There's not much we can do for a shock like this," the doctor had said. "She may come out of it, or she may not. Only time will tell." Time. Zéolie wasn't sure how much of that any of them really had.

"She's here," Zéolie said just before the carriage pulled up in front of the house.

Louis looked at her strangely but said nothing. Odd things were almost normal now. Going to the front door, he motioned for Zéolie to stay back not willing to take any chances with her safety. Pulling aside the corner of a lace curtain in the foyer window, he looked outside.

In the street, Vernand climbed down from the carriage and flipped the side steps down before opening the door for Mama Nell. He took her hand and she seemed to pour out of the carriage and up the steps to the house. Louis absently wondered if the woman's feet actually touched the ground at all as he opened the front door for her. Vernand gave a nod to Louis, swung back into the driver's seat and went to secure the carriage before joining them.

Mama Nell crossed the threshold and took a short, shallow breath. Zéolie knew she felt the tremor, too. Shaking off the strange sensation with a toss of her head, the priestess glided over to Zéolie and grasped both of her pale hands in her soft caramel ones. "You're lookin' a sight better than the last time I saw you, cherie. How're you feelin'?"

Zéolie smiled at her aunt. "Better. Thank you for everything you've done for me."

Mama Nell dismissed the formal gratitude with a wave of her hand. "Nonsense. I jus' wish I could've done more..." Her voice trailed off and Zéolie wondered if the priestess was thinking about Angelie, too. "But we can't stand here thinkin' 'bout all that," Mama Nell said after a moment. "We got work to do."

"Let's go to the parlor," Louis suggested. "I'll light some lamps and see if I can find something to drink."

There was really no reason to light lamps this early in the day, but Zéolie knew Louis was trying to find something to do to be helpful in a strange new world for him. Whatever they were up against wasn't likely to be hiding in the shadows of her parlor to be chased away by a kerosene lamp. "Thank you, Louis. There should be some brandy on the sideboard by the desk."

Louis set to work on the lamps and drinks while Zéolie and Mama Nell settled into the parlor chairs. Once again Zéolie was struck by the graceful movements of her aunt. Everything about her was balanced, completely controlled, yet effortlessly natural. As Mama Nell sat in the chaise and curled long legs under her skirt, she leaned her turbaned head back and closed her eyes. Far from appearing sleepy, she seemed in a heightened awareness of her surroundings, absorbing every nuance of the energy around her. Finally, she said, "We'll work in here as much as we can. Vernand'll bring everythin' in once he's got the horse and carriage taken care of."

Zéolie knew Mother Micheaux said there was much work to be done, but she wasn't expecting the mother superior to endorse, much less suggest, the aid of the priestess. She had also been very tight-lipped about what the work was. "Forgive me," Zéolie began, "but Mother Micheaux didn't explain much to me about all of this. She was leaving that to you."

Mama Nell nodded. "An' she was right, cherie. The less the Ursulines are involved, the safer they are. She's prob'ly already done too much." All three were thinking the same thing. The mother superior knew too much and was in danger of incurring Solène's wrath. While Mother Micheaux hadn't defied and faced down Solène like Angelie, she was helping them to bring her down in other ways. "Mother Micheaux knows the danger she's in, but she's smart to keep as much distance between the sisters an' Solène." Mama Nell paused for a moment and ran the fringe of a scarf through her long slender fingers. "Besides, we should let the innocents stay innocent of the ways of the old faith. Let 'em find their joy an' peace in their prayers an' piety." The priestess took the glass of brandy from Louis with a clink of her many bracelets, swirling it gently around the glass before taking a sip. With a slow release of her breath, she relaxed into the warmth of the drink. "There's demons to be faced an' the prayers of the pious won't be enough."

Louis found a seat at an angle from the front window so that he could keep an eye on the street for danger without seeming rude to the women. "We've all seen what this demon woman can do. How do we face an enemy we can't see and whose madness makes her impossible to predict? How do we find her Achilles' heel?"

Mama Nell gave him a motherly smile, her mossy eyes twinkling. "Now, Louis, before we can go after Solène, we have to teach Zéolie to defend herself."

"You're welcome to anything we have here. What do you need?" Zéolie asked.

"There's magic in the everyday things if you know how to use 'em. Herbs, oils, candles. Vernand'll bring my books an' get a few things from the market we'll need to get started. I can teach you how to make candle dressin's, powders, potions, an' oils. Even how to use the energy around you," she paused and looked at Zéolie, "safely."

Zéolie gave her aunt a sheepish grin at the pointed statement, then a cloud settled over her eyes with the memories of that night washing over her. "Safely. I don't know what came over me," she said barely above a whisper. There had been little conversation with Zéolie about that night and the nights of oblivion that followed it. Those who needed to know what happened did, except for Zéolie after her collapse. No one could bring themselves to broach the subject with her, and she didn't ask. There was a jumble of emotions that competed for her attention. Grief and guilt did battle in her heart every waking moment. Solène seemed to feed on her pain, growing more brazen in her verbal onslaughts the more Zéolie dwelt on the heartache of that memory. "I was so angry. So hurt. All she ever did was try to help me. I couldn't—I couldn't just let her die like that. But it was too much power."

Mama Nell leaned forward and put a reassuring hand on Zéolie's knee. "You followed your instinct, cherie, but you didn't know how to control it. I can teach you a lot of things, but for controllin' that power of yours, you're gonna need Camille. Louis, I need to know if you're willin' to go along with what I ask you to do for Zéolie's sake, even if it seems crazy?"

Louis nodded with a shrug. "I'm not sure that anything will seem crazy anymore."

"Alright, then. Tonight, we're gonna see if we can't build us a bridge between Zéolie and Camille."

"You mean a séance?" Louis asked.

Mama Nell shook her head, earrings glinting in the lamplight. "Not exactly. In a séance, you don't know who'll decide to visit an' we need to make sure we're talkin' to Camille. If you're goin' to reach 'er, you need to open a channel. Sometimes it's as simple as holdin' somethin' in your hand that once belonged to a person. Other times, if that don't work, you gotta get creative." Mama Nell winked at

Zéolie then unfolded herself from the chair and looked toward the door. "Vernand's comin' with the basket."

A second later the back door swung open and footsteps made their way down the hall. Louis looked at Mama Nell and Zéolie who seemed to find nothing strange in the preemptive announcement of the man's arrival. He shrugged as Vernand rounded the corner into the parlor holding a large basket made of woven cattail reeds. It creaked as he set it on the floor in front of Mama Nell. She ran her finger down Vernand's arm and smiled warmly at him as he straightened up. Brushing the back of her slender fingers on his ebony cheek, she thanked him.

Louis kept watch while Mama Nell spent the afternoon blessing and cleansing the house. Zéolie followed in her footsteps like a confused shadow watching every action and word trying hopelessly to absorb it all. Windows and thresholds were washed with a mixture of water, herbs, and other foul-smelling things Zéolie didn't want to know about that would purge restless spirits. Murmuring chants and prayers in words Zéolie couldn't understand, the priestess wafted smoldering herbs in the corners of each room—especially Julien's. Memories of the night her hell began washed over Zéolie like a storm surge as she stood on the threshold of her father's bedroom. Mama Nell held up a graceful hand to her. "Stay here. This room holds too much darkness for you yet." With a grateful smiile, Zéolie waited in the hall for Mama Nell to work through the ritual in the one room she couldn't bear to set foot in again.

After a cleansing with herbs and smoke, the women set to work sweeping the floors starting in the back of the house, from the rears of the rooms toward the doors, then finally brushing everything out of the front door as Louis stood between them and any danger that might be outside. "When we sweep the floors," Mama Nell explained, handing Zéolie a broom made from frayed twigs bound with cord, "we're pushin' bad energy out to make room for the good. It gives spirits with bad intentions less darkness to feed on. Less to work with. We strip some of the power from 'em while invitin' in safe energy. Once we cleanse the house, we'll call on the loa to send help an' spiritual protection for you."

Knowledge of the loa from Voodoo practice wasn't new to her, even if she didn't know much about them. Many of the slaves and gens de couleur had worked the loa into the Catholic faith in the city making the line between the two blurry at best. The loa bore a striking similarity to many of the saints, except for their love of human vices and tendency toward the unexpected. Unlike the saints, there were some with more nefarious intentions, along the lines of the Greco-Roman gods. Understanding which ones you were petitioning was important since it was easy enough for a person to end up on the wrong side of a spiteful spirit instead of a beneficial protector. Zéolie wasn't sure she was ready to embrace this exotic faith, but knew that if she wanted to end this, she would need as much help as she could get. Saint or loa, it didn't matter to her.

Louis, who had been silent through the cleansing, asked, "Will all of this keep Solène out of the house?"

Mama Nell lowered her beautiful eyes and shook her head. "No. She's stronger'n this."

"Then what's the point? Why did we go through all this?" Zéolie asked.

The priestess propped the twig broom against a doorframe and stretched her back. "To take as much of the negative out of the house we can. To give 'er less to work with if she decides to strike."

Louis ran his hands through his hair as he tried to understand. "She feeds off the energy around us? Around her?"

"That's right. An' if she's only got good energy to work with, it keeps her darkness from bein' able to take hold as easy. We damn sure don't wanna give 'er any ammunition." She picked up the broom and went back to her sweeping as if it all made perfect sense.

Zéolie and Louis exchanged glances and confused shrugs, but neither pressed the priestess for more.

Shadows grew long between the French Quarter houses as the sun set in splashes of color. Warm golden light crept around the edges of the curtains before fading into cooler blues and grays. As the last of the color stole through the windows, Mama Nell declared the house clear at last. She was as thorough as she could be, leaving nothing to chance. The final step was a ritual cleansing of their own bodies with sage smoke and a trickling of herb water over their heads than ran unchecked down their limbs onto the wood planked floor. Most of what the priestess did was lost on Zéolie who struggled to retain so much information at once. One thing she was sure of was that she'd never be able to repeat the process on her own without Mama Nell's help.

Vernand brought in a tray of food and drink, setting it down on a small table. Fruit, cheese, and some fresh baguettes and a pitcher of water with lemons sliced in it. Zéolie wondered where he had found the meal since the food in the kitchen must have spoiled in all the time the house had been empty. If he left to get it, he'd gone and returned without her noticing.

"Now," Mama Nell began, pulling a chair up to the table, "we need to get ready for tonight's work." With that, she put her hands out with her palms flat over the tray. Bracelets swayed on her wrists clinking softly, and rings glittered in the lamplight. Closing her eyes, she tilted her head to the heavens, and blessed the simple meal. It was a long day of work that took a toll on the four of them and the meal passed in relative silence. Each seemed lost in their own thoughts, only saying a few polite things now and again.

Zéolie's thoughts were never her own anymore. Her mother's voice was ever-present—taunting, teasing, singing. Solène's snide anger was more welcome to Zéolie than her attempts at sweetness. She could brace herself against the attacking voice, but there was something about the forced kindness that made Zéolie's skin crawl. That was the mood Solène was in at supper, although she could never maintain it very long. Mocking always slipped into the sweetest of her ramblings. "Mon petit chou, let me teach you. You are *mine. My* child. She can't teach you anything. What does *she* know? She's nothing but a *bastard*! Armand's little *bastard girl by his Haitian whore*!" Once in a while, Solène would realize the vileness in what she said and try to take it back. Other times she'd just cackle and sing. Zéolie wondered how much of it was madness and how much of the verbal onslaught was intended to wear her down.

After the small meal was cleared, Mama Nell stood and untied one of the scarves at her waist. She shook it open and let the shimmering material float like colored mist onto the small table. The same one where Zéolie, Celeste, and Lisette played tarot the week before her father died. It seemed apropos that this was the table used for contacting Camille.

"Louis, turn those lights down for me, cherie," Mama Nell asked without taking her eyes away from the table she was setting the basket on. Without a word, Louis went around the room turning the keys in the hurricane lamps to a low blue flame. Darkness settled heavy on the room as the last lamp was dimmed. Cautious foreboding lurked in the shadows despite the cleansing. From the reed basket, the priestess took out a candle, a small jar, a black stone bowl, and a cloth pouch then set them in the center of the table. Next, she produced a corked bottle of salt and a dark amber vial of what looked to Zéolie like dirt. Mama Nell set the vial of dirt to one side, opened the salt and sprinkled it around the table. "Pull your chairs up to the table but don't touch it," she instructed. Zéolie, Louis, and Vernand did as they were told. Mama Nell held her hands out in front of her with her palms out, elbows close to her sides. She closed her eyes and murmured something as she slowly pushed her hands out in front of her, straightening her arms. "This creates a safe space in the energy aroun' me an' pushes that safety aroun' all of you," Mama Nell explained. Then, she opened her arms wide to the side and tilted her head back praying to whoever it was she needed to invoke. It seemed more open and less penitent than the bowed heads, clasped hands, and kneeling she was used to in Mass. The priestess' way was an honest invitation for the spirits, saints, and loa to come as welcome guests to her table.

After her prayer, Mama Nell opened the jar and took a sip of the liquid inside before pouring it slowly into the black bowl. It smelled fresh and clean. "Rainwater," Zéolie whispered.

Mama Nell's burgundy lips curled into a satisfied grin. "Good girl, but this is even better—moon water. Rainwater bathed in the light of the waxin' crescent moon. A moon of opportunities to come; a moon of growth an' possibility."

"A moon of change," Zéolie added.

Mama Nell struck a match and lit the candle in the center of the table. Flickering light danced on the gently moving surface of the moon water. The candle in the center of the table sputtered and popped, then calmed to a steady swaying flame. Zéolie watched it mesmerized for a moment. In the candlelight, there was warmth and peace. There was also power. It was hypnotic to one who had lost all those things.

As Zéolie watched the flame, Mama Nell opened the cloth bag, hesitating a moment before reaching inside. Louis watched the priestess' face change as she touched the object within. Her breath caught in her throat, and he was sure he saw tears welling up in her mossy green eyes. Blinking them back and taking a deep breath to steel her nerves again, she pulled something out of the bag. "Hold out your hand, cherie," she told Zéolie pulling her out of the peaceful trance the flame had put her in. "We've got to make sure we get to Camille, so we depend on a little sympathetic magic an' use somethin' to help connect to 'er."

Zéolie opened her hand over the table and watched as Mama Nell held her closed hand above hers. Solène had been singing one of her ridiculously sweet songs all day as they worked but stopped abruptly as Mama Nell opened her hand and let her treasure trickle into Zéolie's palm. Bead by wooden bead, a rosary slipped through Mama Nell's graceful fingers ending finally in a silver crucifix. As the crucifix fell into her hand, Zéolie felt a surge of electricity race up her arm. Pulling back from the pain, she almost dropped the rosary, but Mama Nell's lightning fast hand closed over hers. "Hold it, hold it tight," the priestess ordered. "Feel everythin' that comes to you."

What came to her was almost more than Zéolie could bear. A raging torrent of thoughts, emotions, and sensations. A chaotic rush from joy to pain, fear to fury, power to helplessness. Hair on her arms and neck stood on end from the energy pulsing through her, and still Mama Nell held her hand tightly closed. Solène shrieked and raged wildly above the tumultuous din in Zéolie's mind. Zéolie tugged hard, trying to free her hand and its powerful contents from Mama Nell, but her aunt refused to let go. "Focus, Zéolie!" Nell barked. "Find somethin' happy an' grab it with everythin' you've got!"

Zéolie's body was wracked with convulsions as she tried to control the turbulence inside. Louis jumped up to help her, but Mama Nell yanked him back into his chair with her free hand and gave him a warning look, eyes narrowed and harder than he had ever seen them. All he could do was watch helplessly as the woman he loved was contorted and manipulated by something terrible and unseen. He turned wide frightened eyes on Vernand, who was sitting calmly across the table as if none of this was happening. *How can he just sit there like that?* Louis thought. Panic grew in him as he watched Zéolie go pale. His gut twisted, and hands shook watching her being tortured. Just as he thought he couldn't let this go on any longer, she began to relax, and color returned to her face. She was taking control of whatever it was. A serene strength washed over her, and Louis' fear slowly abated.

"That's it, cherie." Mama Nell eased her grip on Zéolie's hand and gently opened her fingers. Raising the amber vial, Mama Nell sprinkled dirt over the rosary then folded Zéolie's fingers back over it. Louis watched as Zéolie's brow wrinkled in confusion for a moment, then softened into a slight smile. "What do you see?" her aunt whispered.

Zéolie's eyes were still closed, but she answered, "Camille." She raised her other hand in front of her. "She's here. Just in front of me."

"What's she doin'?"

"Smiling at me." The vision in Zéolie's mind drowned out the chaos and shrieking of Solène, not with noise, but with a quiet rustling sound of fluttering cloth, like ship's sails in the wind. Floating just in front of her was her grandmother. Camille's long shining silver hair was loose and flowing, just like her dress, and seemed to glimmer as it swirled behind her. She didn't seem transparent like Zéolie would have expected of a spirit, but instead rippled as if she were underwater and Zéolie was on the surface looking at her.

Camille smiled at her granddaughter and spoke, "I'm so proud of you, Zéolie. You're stronger than you realize, cherie." Her voice echoed and shimmered in the space around them.

"I don't understand how you can say that. She's taken so much, and I couldn't stop her. Angelie was the only one who could and she's..." Zéolie couldn't say it.

Camille smiled warmly at Zéolie. "She's safe now. And at peace. Remember, Solène can't take you by force. You'd have to go to her willingly. And if you do, there's nothing I, or anyone else, can do to help you."

"She tortures me. Sometimes I'm so tired of fighting her that I almost..."

"I know, cherie, I know, but you are *not* Solène's. You are your own. Tu appartiens à toi-même."

The vision began to fade, becoming less solid as the rippled image dissolved. Edges of Camille's shimmering gown began to fray, and the image eventually disintegrated into a sparkling mist before vanishing completely. Solène's voice returned as the quiet faded with Camille. "*You are mine, cherie.*" her mother hissed. "*Nothing will change that!*"

Zéolie squeezed her eyes shut to block out her mother's anger as she opened her hand. Slowly she opened her eyes and looked across the table at Mama Nell. "How did you do that?" she asked hoarsely. "How did you get Camille to come to me?"

Mama Nell shook her head. "I gave you the tools. Angelie's rosary an' the dust from Camille's grave. That's all. You opened the channel yourself. An' she's been wantin' to see you, which helped. They've got to want to come to us on their own."

Angelie's rosary. The words hit Zéolie like a brick wall. Tears trickled down her face with the grief of that horrible night. She ran the mahogany beads of the rosary through her fingers feeling the energy tingle with each one. At the end of the short chain hung the silver crucifix. Zéolie's finger touched the body of Christ and wondered what He would think of all of this. Turning it over in her hand, she saw an inscription on the back of the cross and blinked back tears to read the tiny words:

Tu appartiens à toi-même.

CHAPTER
TWELVE

Vernand's knock on the bedroom door was almost imperceptible. "Mademoiselle?" he called softly.

Mama Nell uncurled her legs from the chaise she had been sleeping in and opened the door. "She's still sleepin'. Let 'er rest, mon amour." The priestess slid her graceful arms under his and around his strong back, pulling him close. Her head rested on his chest for a long moment. Standing there on the threshold, she seemed to be drinking in strength from him. Without a word, Vernand stood holding her to him and kissed her forehead gently.

Mama Nell pulled back and kissed his cheek, then his lips, softly and fleeting. He looked into her gentle eyes and whispered, "There's been a letter come for Zéolie. It's from Madame Marchon. Her man brought it by a few minutes ago."

Mama Nell nodded. "Soon as she's up." Vernand kissed her forehead again and disappeared down the hallway. The priestess sank back into the chaise and watched her niece sleep for a few moments. Zéolie laid awake for hours until Mama Nell finally brewed her a sleeping tea. Even with the sedative herbs, the girl passed a difficult night. After the encounter with Camille, the mental onslaught from

Solène had been brutal. The witch was getting more desperate to get her hands on Zéolie before the girl was strong enough to resist. Mama Nell knew time was running out and there was no guarantee that Zéolie would ever be able to face down her mother. She also knew they had no choice. Solène would keep killing until she got what she wanted.

THE LETTER from Madame Marchon was hastily scribbled. Her usual careful even script seemed so erratic that Zéolie almost doubted at first that she had actually written it.

Darling Zéolie,

The last thing I want to do is leave you at a time like this, but Louis is right. As long as Solène is on the rampage, the girls are in danger. They know too much to be safe from her and Celeste is too weak to take any more abuse at the hands of that demon woman. All we can hope is that her reach is confined to the city and the girls will be safe somewhere else. You understand, of course, that I can't tell you where we are going., but you will never be out of our thoughts. We love you so much, cherie, and know that we'll soon be together again.

READING THE STRAIGHTFORWARD NOTE, Zéolie was reassured it was written by Madame Marchon. Celeste and Lisette signed their names below their mother's and Zéolie could see tear stains at the bottom of the page. Letting the letter fall in her lap, she leaned back on the headboard of her bed, and closed her eyes. They were right, of course. Madame Marchon and Louis knew best. They weren't safe as long as her mother was on a rampage, but Zéolie doubted that anywhere was out of Solène's reach. No one she held dear was safe anymore. She knew Louis warned the women she loved so dearly about Solène's growing strength hoping he could save them.

"This has to end," she said to herself.

Solène's laugh rumbled up from the depths of Zéolie's mind, clearly pleased that she managed to remove yet another obstacle to getting to Zéolie even though she had nothing to do with sending the Marchons away. One by one, the walls around Zéolie were being taken down leaving fewer and fewer layers of protection from the gathering force of her mother's rage.

Zéolie dressed and found Mama Nell in the courtyard setting small pots out in a wheel pattern. In a corner by one of the brick walls were plants of all sorts, clay pots, and several baskets of rich delta soil waiting to be placed in the pattern. Morning air in the courtyard hung heavy with humidity, but the walls of the house cast just enough shade to make it bearable. Hibiscus blossoms bloomed happily oblivious to the terror in the household. The center of the courtyard was adorned with a three-tiered fountain that bubbled and dribbled peacefully. Somewhere under the lily pads in the basin, a frog croaked softly. The fountain itself served as the hub of the wheel with pots branching out in twelve directions from it. "Can I do something to help?" Zéolie asked her aunt.

Mama Nell stood up straight and arched her back like a cat stretching on a lazy afternoon. Brushing the dirt from her hands, she handed a stack of pots to Zéolie. "You can help me put these out an' we'll get the plantin' done."

"Where should they go?'

"You see the wheel takin' shape 'round the fountain? There's twelve spokes on the wheel - one for each sign of the zodiac. If we plant things in the right sign, they'll grow strong with the powers of that sign—good or bad." She winked at Zéolie. "Each has its usefulness."

By dusk, the wheel was complete, the pots making the outline with spaces in the spokes for the women to go in and tend them. Each plant was carefully placed and blessed while Mama Nell explained what traits they had that aligned them to the signs and what each could be used for. Some plants had rather mundane uses while others were strange and dangerous. Zéolie tried to remember as much as Mama Nell would teach her, but the task was overwhelming, and she doubted her own ability to raise the plants to their full potency. Delia had always tended the flowers and kitchen herb garden. Zéolie had no idea what she was doing when it came to this sort of thing.

Solène took to singing a lewd drinking song that resembled something sailors would sing as they worked. She grew louder when she got to the bawdy chorus, clearly amused at the references to buxom women and love-starved men. Zéolie wasn't sure if she preferred the obnoxious singing to the rambling tirades or not. It was also difficult to tell if Solène was less dangerous when she was happy, or if her happiness was because she was up to something heinous. Zéolie desperately hoped for the former.

In the fading gray light, Mama Nell let the fountain rinse the dirt from her strong caramel hands then dried them on her skirt. "That's enough for today," she said taking a satisfied look around. "Now, back inside. There's time for one more lesson."

As the sun set, the two women moved the lessons back around the small table in the parlor. Mama Nell placed a white candle in the center and small colored ones around it. "What are we doing now?" asked Zéolie.

"Candle magic. Each color represents somethin' else. Some priestesses'll tell you that color means everythin', but I never set much store in that. Magic's only as good as the intention behind it, so use whatever feels right."

"How does it work?" Zéolie asked.

Mama Nell lit the center candle, sat back in her chair, and crossed her long legs. "Close your eyes an' think about what you wanna know. Candles can send magic out in the smoke an' flame or draw it to you like a moth."

Zéolie closed her eyes and tried to clear her mind. She knew what she wanted to know but knew any thoughts of Louis only brought taunting from her mother. Instead, she focused on what she had been trying to escape for so long. Solène. Rumbles of laughter began to swell in the depths of her mind, but Zéolie knew that if she were going to face down her mother, she needed to know what to be looking for. She had seen her once in a windowpane in the moonlight, but it was only a glimpse. She wanted a good look at her enemy.

Opening her eyes, she looked at the candles in front of her. "The black one."

Mama Nell's eyes narrowed. "You sure?"

"I'm sure."

"Dark candles are for dark purposes. What're you lookin' for, cherie?"

Zéolie looked into her aunt's eyes levelly. "I want to see her. I've heard enough of Solène. I need to see her."

Mama Nell shook her head. "That's a dangerous road you're on. You're openin' a door to her world that's best left shut. Don't invite her in, Zéolie."

Solène's laughter turned to cursing. *To hell with her, Zéolie. That damned swamp rat can't tell you what to do. Light the candle, cherie.*

Zéolie took a deep breath and held her hand out over the colored candles. Her palm tingled as it passed over the black candle and she felt a pulling from the center of her hand as if there was a thread running through her hand tugging it down. She resisted, but only a little. Before she was even aware of what she was doing, the wick of the black candle was in the flame of the spirit candle in the center of the table. As the wick caught, Zéolie was thrown violently back in her chair. The black candle, still gripped in her shaking hand, began to drip wax down her arm scalding her skin, but she couldn't let it go. She was pinned to the chair that was balancing precariously on the back legs. Mama Nell watched in horror as Zéolie's head lolled backwards and her dark eyes rolled back in their sockets. A foul-smelling sulfurous wind began to whip through the room and laughter reverberated off the walls, but still the candle flames held steady. Suddenly, the black candle flame leapt wildly and showered Zéolie in sparks.

"You opened the door, child!" Mama Nell shrieked over the roaring of the wind and laughter. "You've got to fight 'er. *Don't let 'er in!*" As the words left the priestess' mouth, her lips were sealed shut and a hard slap landed across her face nearly knocking her out of the chair. Red welts raised on her smooth caramel cheek. The witch then turned her attention back to her daughter who was struggling to let go of the black candle that was spitting and sparking in her hand. As Solène focused her torment on Zéolie, Mama Nell reached into the scarves at her waist frantically trying to get something out.

Inside Zéolie's head, a storm raged. Heat surged up one arm and icy shards seemed to be stabbing the other. She shook the hand with the candle madly sending hot wax splattering across the floor and table, but her fingers would not release it. Focusing on the other hand, she managed to free it from its grip on the arm of the chair and began to claw at her own fingers clutching the black candle. It was no use.

She could see swirling images in her mind, but none of them clearly. They all seemed to be veiled in the shimmering heat of fire and smoke. Solène laughed at her and teased her, playing with strands of her hair and stroking her face, but always as though she were behind her. *Come to me, cherie. Come to me and you'll see me. I'll show you a world you can only imagine. Power beyond your wildest dreams. You can have anything you want. My precious girl.*

"*No!*" Zéolie screamed into the roaring wind. As she screamed, Zéolie felt something being thrust into the palm of her free hand. Gritty and smooth at the same time. As she wrapped her fingers around it, the images changed and the temperature around her dropped. Suddenly, she was looking through a hazy glass at a silvery light blazing the in flames in her mind. The roaring of the wind and cackling of her mother was muffled and distant. Silver light began to shift and surge forward into the darkness before it, pushing it deeper and deeper into the recesses. With every push, Zéolie felt lighter and cooler. The burning and stabbing stopped, and a curious calm washed over her mind and body. "Camille," she whispered. Her own voice sounded far away, lost in the muffled chaos.

Silver flashed in a blinding light and Zéolie felt herself falling forward as the chair settled back onto all four legs. She was free. Camille set her free, but how? Then she remembered something was in her hand. The black candle lay in a puddle of wax on the floor, remnants dripping from her fingertips. Her other hand slowly opened to reveal the dusty rosary.

Zéolie looked across the table at Mama Nell who gave her a small exhausted smile. "You alright, child?" her aunt asked.

Zéolie nodded, but truthfully wasn't. Her hands trembled as her mother showered her with curses and taunts. She held her head in pain from the attack, as vileness spewed from the witch who was so close to getting what she wanted. Color drained from Zéolie's face as Solène raged on. Her mother was becoming stronger, countering every advance in strength Zéolie made, and becoming harder and harder to resist.

Mama Nell began burning a bundle of dried sage to try to cleanse the space of the black energy of the witch. As the earthy smoke curled towards the ceiling, she chanted and sang to call on the intercession of the loa. Zéolie didn't understand the words but prayed desperately for them to work. Flame dancing on the white candle surged higher as spirits gathered around it. For the first time, Zéolie could feel them. She couldn't see them or hear them, but there was a gathering presence she couldn't ignore. Power built. Energy shifted. Solène continued her tirade, but the voice seemed more distant now. Something was pushing her mother back into the recesses of Zéolie's consciousness and she began to relax. As she did, she became acutely aware of how exhausted she was. Her whole body ached. Wax burns on her hand and arm stung. As she gazed at the candle flame burning strong and steady in the center of the table, her eyelids began to get heavy.

Mama Nell took her hand, led her to the settee, and laid her down. Zéolie would sleep while the priestess and the loa kept vigil over her throughout the night.

CHAPTER
THIRTEEN

As the sun eased over the horizon, Mama Nell was able to cease the chanting and spell work she had done all night. Her niece had slept, but the priestess hadn't. There wasn't time for that now, and she wasn't tired anyway. Usually, trances exhausted her, but she felt refreshed as she finally released this one. Something was different this time. Whatever it was, the priestess was grateful for it. There was work to do.

Zéolie's lessons continued with the plants as they ground dried herbs hanging from a wooden grid in the kitchen ceiling. The kitchen in the rear of the courtyard was small, but welcoming. Fire glowed in the cooking fireplace and a cast iron pot hung at the ready over the coals. Under fogged over windows, a long wooden bench stretched almost the full length of the room. It was here that they spread out the work of the day. Taking each bunch of herbs down, Mama Nell explained how the herb was harvested and dried. The priestess treated each tiny leaf with reverence. Every deft movement of her fingers was liquid grace. "You gotta respect the magic, no matter what. It might seem like a slow way to do things," the priestess explained as she plucked a shriveled leaf from its stem, "but harvestin' their power correctly adds to the energy it possesses. Disrespect that an' the plant'll respond."

Once all the herbs were harvested and stripped of their tough stems, Mama Nell set a large mortar and pestle on the table. A heady aroma filled the small kitchen. As they worked, it got even stronger. Crushing and grinding the herbs forced the plants to release their essences and Mama Nell showed her how to mix them, combining the powers for different purposes. The air in the kitchen was rich with earthy smells bringing memories of the smells from moments of semi-consciousness in the swamp. As they worked and Mama Nell chanted and sang, more of those slivers of memories made sense. The priestess had been nursing Zéolie back to health with the old magic all that time.

"If I have to face her, there won't be time for all of this, will there?" Zéolie asked cautiously, trying not to offend her aunt.

The priestess shook her head. "No, cherie, you'll have to use your own power for that. But, if we can use these herbs to ward off any evil that might be lurkin' around you otherwise, there's less to drain what precious strength you got."

Zéolie began to see that there was more to this strange new mystical world than she could hope to learn in a lifetime, much less in the time she could feel rapidly diminishing. Her mother was growing more relentless and Zéolie could feel the noose tightening.

Undaunted, Mama Nell continued her work. "Nature gives us so much to work with an' few notice power surroundin' them every day. Take these leaves," she said holding a bundle of a deep green plant. "Inside's a powerful oil, if you know how to get to it." She glided over to the corner of the kitchen. There was something under a large tablecloth that seemed to be a mass of odd angles. Gently, Mama Nell removed the cloth and folded it. What she revealed was something strange, but somehow familiar. As Zéolie looked at the contraption of scraps of metal welded together, she realized it was something she had seen at the swamp cabin.

"What is it?" Zéolie asked quietly.

"It's a still," Mama Nell answered. "Like makin' alcohol, you can use a still like this one to pull oils from the plants." Taking a smoldering coal from the cooking fire, she lit the flame on the little still. "Fill this part with water," she instructed pointing to a reservoir above the flame. "Now, put those leaves here." The small mesh basket looked similar to baskets used to steam seafood. Zéolie carefully laid the leaves in the basket that was suspended above the water reservoir. Mama Nell closed up the section of the still and poured cold water into the condenser.

"What now?" Zéolie asked.

"Now, we wait," she replied placing a small glass jar under a pipe on the end of the still. Mama Nell went back to the mortar and pestle leaving the still to extract the oils on its own.

All morning, Solène had been content to sing the bawdy drinking song and giggle to herself. Zéolie expected a renewal of the cursing and raging from the night before, but it seemed her mother was in a better mood. Something about that unnerved Zéolie, but she couldn't think about that with so much yet to learn.

Memories from oblivion came back to her even more as Mama Nell showed her how to apply the oils she already made and taught her the chants and songs that added intention and power to them. All things she had done to restore Zéolie's health after her magical misfire.

In all the lessons with the herbs and oils, Mama Nell talked of harnessing energy around her to serve whatever needs she had. Control was vital if Zéolie was going to survive an attack from Solène. There was no way she could survive another loose cannon release of energy like the explosion in the swamps. Before each blessing or application of the spells, Mama Nell would work her through the process of grounding herself and feeling the energy flowing through her in different directions. The sense of energy flow was the source of her power and Zéolie had to feel it as naturally as her own skin.

"Close your eyes," Mama Nell instructed in a soft rich voice. "Feel the ground beneath your feet an' see your roots windin' deep into the earth below you like a tree. There's strength in 'em to hold you strong an' steady." Zéolie closed her eyes and saw roots spreading from the soles of her feet through the rich black soil underground. She could smell the earthiness, like old wood and dried leaves, as she inhaled deeply. Releasing her breath, she saw the roots split and spread deep and wide beneath her adding stability and taking the fear from her core deep into the ground. Nell's words seemed to be coming to her from far away now. "Breathe in only those things that'll give you strength an' power. Breathe out an' release those things that won't." Zéolie breathed in deeply and released it slowly. Tingling stung her hands as energy collected there for the work she was doing. Holding her palms over the mortar and pestle, she could almost see it flowing into the herbs.

By NIGHTFALL, firelight glinted off the amber bottles of a long row of herb mixtures, oils, and tinctures lined up on the kitchen workbench. "Now," Mama Nell said holding a vial up to the light turning it slowly in her sender fingers, "we put 'em to use." Mama Nell gathered a few of the small corked vials in a scarf, tying the corners into a pouch. Bottles clinked softly as they nestled against each other.

Zéolie walked behind her towards the house feeling more like she was being carried on a wave in the wake of the grace and strength her aunt possessed. Mama Nell was always straight and tall, standing confidently but never rigidly. There was always a fluid element to any movement she made. It was almost as if the swamp water she was raised among was in her very blood. As if the water moved through her body and carried her along. Even if Zéolie didn't know what her aunt was, she would have known there was something ethereal about this woman.

Going inside, Mama Nell found the reed basket Vernand brought from her cabin and opened it. Taking out several candles in different sizes and colors, she once more arranged them on the parlor table. Next to them, she placed the vials from the kitchen and a small silver knife.

"By now you know the power of the earth an' what it gives us to work with. You saw yourself how that energy can be harnessed." Zéolie nodded. So much information was coming at her at once. Her fractured mind was like a sieve; most of what Zéolie was told slipped away from her and only a few things lodged in her memory. "Sit down, cherie." Mama Nell put a white pillar candle and the knife in front of Zéolie and got paper, quill pen, and ink for herself. Slowly, she began to draw a small symbol on the paper. "There's also power in words an' symbols, like this one," she said pointing at the shape with a graceful caramel finger. "It's a sigil. A sort of secret code wrapped up in a shape made from a single line. They all mean different things. Each of us creates the ones that speak to us. Some're simple sigils like this one, but others can be made more intricately. Some're made from patterns an' systems passed down over the generations. They evolve with us as we need 'em."

Mama Nell picked up the knife and handed it to Zéolie. It was delicate, but a good weight. Easy to hold and manipulate. Lamp light glinted off the blade and, for a split second, she remembered the story Mama Nell told her about the night her mother died but didn't, and the image of her mother holding a knife over her baby - over *her*. Tears began to well up in Zéolie's eyes and she blinked them back hard. There was no time to dwell on the past and what her father had to do. "It's beautiful," she said turning the knife over in her hand.

The priestess' burgundy lips curled at the corners in a wistful smile. "That it is. Special, too." She paused for a moment, seemingly lost in thought, before coming back to the work at hand. "Symbols can work for us in lots of ways. One way is to draw 'em on paper or leaves an' burn 'em to release the intention through the smoke. Another way is to carve 'em into a candle to dedicate it to what we're using the candle to do. As the candle burns, the intention's released."

Mama Nell laid the gleaming blade gently on the table, then handed one of the candles to Zéolie. "Hold it in your hand, movin' it around a bit. Let it tell you where to carve."

Zéolie held the candle in her left hand and turned it with her right. As she did, she let her hand hover slightly above the side of the candle. At first, she couldn't feel anything, but after another turn, she felt a pull from the center of her palm towards the candle. It was slight, but definitely there. "Here," she said. Mama Nell handed her the knife and Zéolie slowly carved the symbol from the paper into the side of the candle. The sharp blade eased through the wax with little resistance, but the wax never allowed the blade very deep. Unlike Mama Nell and the pen and paper, Zéolie had to lift the knife and turn the blade to make the corners of the sigil. When she finished, she carefully brushed flakes of wax from the design.

"Beautifully done," Mama Nell said. "Now, we consecrate it to the purpose." She laid a piece of paper on the table and sprinkled herbs on it. Next, she opened a vial of oil and poured several drops of it on Zéolie's fingertips. "Start at the bottom an' pull your fingers up the side of the candle to bring the magic to you. Your purpose determines the direction you move the oil on the candle. To draw somethin' to you, pull the oil towards your body and up the wick. To repel somethin', pull the oil toward the bottom of the candle. State your intention for the spell as you dress the candle with the oil." Zéolie murmured as she pulled her fingertips from the bottom of the candle to the top leaving a shimmering streak of oil with each pass. "Now, take the candle an' hold it at each end. Gently roll it in the herbs." As she did, the herbs clung to the oil on the side of the candle making it look as earthy as it smelled.

With the candle dressed, it was time to bless it and seal the intention by lighting it. Zéolie struck a match and held it to the candle. The flame leapt high when it touched the oil on the wick, popped and sputtered, then went out. Mama Nell's brow wrinkled in thought. "That shouldn't've happened. Try again, but this time speak your intention as you light it."

Zéolie held the match over the wick and said, 'Give me strength to do what needs to be done." The match went out. Something was wrong. "I—I don't understand."

The crucifix on the end of the chain around her neck went ice cold against her skin. Zéolie grabbed it and it shocked her hand. She frantically pulled the chain over her head and dropped it on the table in front of her. "What is it, child?" Mama Nell asked.

"The crucifix. It's like ice, but it shocked me," she answered staring at the rosary.

"Someone's tryin' to tell you somethin'."

"Who?"

"It wouldn't be Angelie with somethin' like this. It's got to be Camille."

Zéolie held her hand out over the crucifix, wanting to feel it, but not touch it. She closed her eyes and felt the warmth and quiet she had felt when she saw Camille. "It *is* Camille. I can feel her now. But what am I doing wrong?"

Mama Nell thought back through what Zéolie said. "Your intention needs work. She don't want you to set the wrong one. You see, when it comes to magic, you got to be specific. All you asked for was 'the strength to do what needs to be done.' For all the magic knows, you just need strength to do the washin'."

Zéolie thought for a moment about what she truly needed strength to do. "I don't know exactly what I need to do to stop her."

"One thing you gotta remember," Mama Nell cautioned. "Be specific in what you *need*, but don't tell the magic *how* to solve your problem. Sometimes problems're solved in ways we can never see comin'."

Zéolie pushed her black hair over her shoulders and out of her way then lit the match again. Taking a deep measured breath, she grounded herself. "Give me strength to do what needs to be done to stop the murderous madness of my mother." The match stayed lit as Zéolie brought it to the candlewick. Fire jumped high and bright as the wick caught and the candle quickly settled into a strong steady flame that gleamed on the crucifix lying on the table. Camille was happy with that one.

"There, now," Mama Nell said, her soft green eyes almost golden in the firelight. "We get signs all the time, but we don't usually notice 'em. Simple things can mean somethin' if you're payin' attention. Of course, we usually let those things slide right by us. But, if somethin' starts to go haywire in your ritual work, then you better listen."

Mama Nell had Zéolie practice "dressin' and blessin'" a few more candles to make sure she fully understood the power of setting her intention clearly. As she practiced, Camille's interference became more infrequent. Soon, the work of the night took a physical toll on Zéolie and she needed to rest. With Camille involved in the lesson, Solène kept her distance, but sang merrily in the background making Zéolie uneasy.

"You go on up to bed, cherie. I'll make your tea." Mama Nell took Zéolie's hands in hers, looked at her neice for a moment, and said softly, "There's so much of your father in you." Solène snorted a laugh at that.

Zéolie smiled at Mama Nell, but it didn't make it to her dark eyes. The weight of her world was becoming harder to carry and she secretly feared that her mother's madness would find its way into her own mind before Zéolie could stop her. She needed sleep badly. And Louis. She knew he would never understand what they were doing, but his presence had a way of steadying her.

CHAPTER

FOURTEEN

Frantic pounding on the door brought Louis out of his troubled sleep with a start. "Who the hell is it?" he yelled at the closed door to his apartment, stalling a minute while he pulled on his pants and lit a candle. As a police officer, he was used to the noise of the Quarter all night and the occasional middle of the night wake-up pounding, but this seemed different. The sound was panicked and fast, and definitely not the firm sharp knock of a fellow officer. With Zéolie back at the house on Dauphine, he abandoned his Ninth Ward cot for his own bed closer to her. His hopes for an uneventful night's sleep were shattered by the banging on the door.

"Please, suh! Open up!" called a small boy. His voice was small and urgent. Opening the door, Louis looked down at the small frightened slave boy in dirty clothes stained with grease spots. A kitchen slave in one of the restaurants, likely. Clutched in his hand was a crumpled piece of paper held straight out to Louis.

"What's this?" Louis asked taking the paper and holding the door wider for the boy to come in.

"A note, suh. Can't read it, but da man said it was fuh you," the boy answered staying rooted to his spot on the outside of the apartment door.

"Come in, boy. I won't hurt you."

The boy nodded and managed a sheepish grin on his grimy dark face. "I know, suh. Thank you." He stepped slowly into the apartment and stood nervously wringing his hands.

Louis went to the kitchen and got a baguette for the boy, who looked half- starved. "Eat this. You earned it." Louis smiled as the boy took the roll and pulled it in half. He stuffed half of it into his pocket for later and devoured the rest. As Louis opened the crumpled paper and began reading the sweat-smeared ink, the smile died on his lips. "Who gave this to you?" he asked sharply.

The startled boy almost choked on his bread. "A dark man, suh. I didn't know 'im, but he warn't a slave like me. Talked too nice fuh dat. Said he knew you an' I betta get dat note to you fas' as I could run."

"Why didn't he bring it to me himself?" Louis asked, his blue eyes narrowing. The officer in him was not going to take something this out of the ordinary on face value.

The frightened boy shrugged. "I dunno, suh. I didn't ask. Sorry, suh. He was in a awful hurry to go."

Louis patted the boy on his curly head. "Thank you. You did good. Go home and get some sleep." The boy nodded, double-checked his pocket for the baguette half, then scurried back out into the night.

Louis reread the note.

Louis,

Get to the cabin as fast as you can. She's got them.

Vernand

It was cryptic to anyone who may have intercepted the note, but Louis knew exactly what it meant.

"*God damn it!*" he cursed. "You're a damned fool for leaving that house, Louis!" he raged at himself as he threw on the closest clothes he could find and took off into the night.

Gas lamps spilled puddles of warm golden glow along the walls of the close-set buildings of the French Quarter. Louis raced in and out of the pools of light and shadow searching for a carriage that would take him to the edge of the swamps north of the city. He'd steal a horse if he had to. Nothing was going to keep him from getting to Zéolie. As crowded as the streets were in the day, there were no carriages in sight in the wee hours of the night. *Damn it! Where the hell is everyone?* The French Quarter seemed strangely vacant and Louis was beginning to panic. His footsteps echoed against the tight buildings as he searched for anyone with a horse. Nothing. Street after street of abandoned lamplight and shadows. Nerves pricked his skin as he realized how unnaturally alone he was. Exasperated, he changed direction and raced toward Canal Street outside the Quarter.

A few blocks further on was the bulky shadow of an open carriage on the side of the street. The horse started when it heard Louis' footsteps on the cobblestones. "Shhh," Louis whispered trying to calm the animal as he approached even as his own heart pounded in his ears. He stroked the animal's strong neck and held the bridle. Horseshoes clicked on the stones underfoot and the leather carriage straps creaked as the horse settled back down. Louis patted it one more time reassuringly. The last thing he needed was for the horse to bolt on him.

In the front of the carriage, swaying with the movements of the horse, was a dark man smelling of alcohol and tobacco. Jostled awake, he pulled his hat off his eyes, and blinked the sleep away. "Help you, monsieur?" he asked thickly.

"I need you to take me north of the city," Louis ordered not wasting time on niceties.

The dark man's eyes widened and the whites of them shone in the gas light. "Now, monsieur? You crazy. You best wait 'til daylight. Can't nothin' good come of goin' out there now."

Louis was losing his patience. "I'm Officer Louis Saucier and I need to get north of the city *right now*. Are you taking me, or am I taking your horse?"

The man immediately snapped to as he jumped down from the driver's seat to hand up his new passenger. "No need for that, monsieur. Officer, I mean. Happy to take you," the man said with an unnecessarily deep bow.

Zéolie's life depended on him getting to Mama Nell's cabin and he was out of options. Louis climbed on the open carriage and the man snapped the whip over the head of the horse. With a lurch as the horse pulled against the harness, the carriage clattered off through the dark streets, the lanterns hanging on the front swinging wildly and throwing strange shadows against the deserted Quarter.

As they raced out of the city, night seemed to close in tight around them. Gas lights on banquettes vanished with candle-lit windows making the world darker and quieter than Louis was comfortable with. Above him, the crescent moon did little to cut through the blackness. What light it did give was shrouded in thin misty clouds washing silver across the night sky. He wished desperately that it was a full moon that could light the landscape and guide him through the swamp to the cabin, but the sliver remained. There was something strangely sinister in the crescent smile of the moon. It seemed to be sneering down at him, mocking him for his Sir Galahad rush through the night and swamp to save his love. It didn't matter that there was nothing he could do to stop Solène.

After what seemed like hours, they slowed to a halt at the edge of the swamp where Louis directed the driver. The horse's ears laid back and it pawed nervously at the dirt road. Even the animal knew this was insane. "This as far as I go, monsieur," the man said quietly. He looked out into the dark swamp teeming with night sounds and danger. "You sure you wanna do this? I still say no good'll come of it."

Louis looked out into the swamp. Somewhere out there was Zéolie. "I sure as hell don't want to, but I have to. It's alright. I've been here before."

The man shrugged and nodded. "If you're set on it, then." He clambered down from the front seat of the hack and steadied the horse as Louis got down. The agitated animal seemed to have more sense about the place than either of the two men. It whinnied and snorted, sniffing the air. Something out there was spooking it.

"This should cover it, I'd think," Louis said handing the man a wad of bills. It would more than cover it, but Louis was hoping the extra would keep the man's mouth shut.

"Thank you, monsieur," the man said taking the money. "I can stay and wait for a while, in case you change your mind, if you want," he added. The man squinted into the marshes and shifted his weight uncomfortably.

It was a nice offer on the surface, but Louis knew he wasn't likely to make good on it. "It's alright. You go on back. I could be a while."

"At least take this with you, monsieur," he said handing Louis one of the lanterns off the front of the carriage. Louis took the dented metal lantern with a grateful smile. The man gave a sharp nod, climbed back into the carriage, and turned the horse around. At the edge of the wilds, Louis stood watching them vanish into the blackness of the night, weak glints of moonlight dancing on the buckles of the reigns.

The swamp exhaled as wind moved over the tops of the cypress trees, beckoning him to come inside. It called to him like a siren's song, daring him to set foot on the boggy ground and make the trek into its black heart. Louis picked out the barely visible path he took several times before. Shadows danced in the flickering of the carriage lantern with each tentative step. As familiar as the place had become, something wasn't right. For a moment, he listened to the swamp. Even the night sounds of the frogs and insects seemed to have gone silent. A breeze moved the reeds and leaves around him, and he could have sworn the wind was whispering. Running his hands through his hair nervously, he made his way deep into the marsh to face his fate wishing desperately he had Vernand to guide him once more. As much as he wanted to race to Zéolie's rescue, he knew better than to go tearing through the dark swamp. Each step must be carefully and precisely placed. Remembering the fate of Angelie, he held the lantern up to anything he wanted to reach up to and push out of his way. Time crawled as he inched his way through the treacherous land. Each second that he struggled in the mire was a second too late that he might be getting to Nell and Zéolie.

WHEN HE FINALLY CAME TO the place where Mama Nell's cabin stood among the cypress, his lantern was sputtering. The oil was almost gone, and the wick was burned dangerously low. There wouldn't be enough to light the way back out. Louis turned the shutter to reduce the glow to a tiny sliver. There was no reason to let Solène to know he was there just yet if she didn't know already. First, he needed to get the lay of the land. With a maniac, there was no telling what she would do, and he wouldn't get a second chance to surprise her.

Light shone through the dirty glass of the priestess' cabin, flickering in the inky blackness of the deep swamp. Slowly, he crept closer and stood under the creaking cypress pilings upon which the small wooden cabin with its vaulted tin roof so precariously rested. Aged and water-worn stilts were slick with green lichen climbing up them from the swamp floor. The same lichen coated the warped bottom steps making them precarious at best. Cold sweat stood out on Louis' forehead as he assessed his surroundings. Every ounce of his intuition whispered to him, *Run! Run for your life!* but he refused to listen. His heart pounded against the wall of his chest so loudly he was sure the witch could hear it. Pushing it aside, Louis listened to the swamp around him. There were no sounds of struggle, no sounds of movement at all. Staying in the shadows away from the light spilling out of the windows, he climbed the stairs, gently testing each one for the slightest creak before putting his full weight on it.

Making it undetected to the top of the steps and the porch, he could see the front door was slightly ajar. Solène hadn't locked them inside. Hair on his neck stood on end. Something was very wrong with all of this. *Why would she leave the door open if she's taken Mama Nell and Zéolie captive? How is she holding them here?* Louis' stomach sank as he pushed possible answers to that back into the depths of his thoughts. Edging his way to the door, he stood flat against the wall so he could see through the crack. There was no movement inside. Stillness. As if the cabin held its breath to see how far he was willing to go. Louis waited and listened. All he could hear was his own heart pounding loudly in his ears. Silently, he drew his gun unsure what it could really do against Solène.

Easing the door open, he braced himself for a response from the witch, but none came. Taking one slow step after another, Louis moved through the threshold. With the cabin being one large room divided by furniture rather than walls, if Solène was inside, she would have seen him by now. And if she could see him, why hadn't she made a move? Louis edged around the room with his back against the wall as much as he could to prevent her from taking him from behind. *Where has she hidden them?* His heart wanted to scream out for the women, but his head kept his emotions in check. This was already suicide. He didn't need to go asking for it.

Looking around the room, there was nothing disturbed. Dust lay in a soft blanket over the vials and books. Cobwebs covered the shelves. Bundles of dried herbs laid carefully on the workbench. Furniture in the same places as his last visit. Surely, Nell and Zéolie would have fought back. There should be signs of a struggle, but nothing was out of place. *Unless they couldn't fight back. What the hell is going on?* As the thought crossed his mind and he lowered his gun, something dropped on the dark floorboards in front of him. It was shiny and wet, just the smallest spot. Leaning over it, he thought at first it must be water from the humidity dripping from the ceiling. It was too thick for that. Tentatively, he put his finger in it and pulled it back. His heart sank and breath rushed out of his lungs. *Blood.* He stumbled back away from the droplet and whipped his gaze up to the ceiling. High above him, hanging from the rafters in the dark shadows of the vaulted roof, was Vernand. His corpse was stripped to the waist and a thin trickle of blood ran from his lips onto the rope around his neck.

Shock and rage collided in his stomach chilling him to his core. "*Solène!*" he growled. "*Show yourself, witch!*"

Laughter, wild and maniacal, filled the cabin and rattled the walls. The cabin door slammed shut behind him. Louis raised his gun but had no target. "Now, now, cherie," Solène's voice was silk. "Let's not begin that way." A cold unseen hand grabbed his arm and wrenched it behind him. The gun burned white hot in Louis' hand and he could smell his flesh burning making him drop the weapon with a roar of pain. "There, now, *that's* better," she crooned. The same unseen force yanked the gun away as he dove for it, then held him face-down on the ground as if there was a knee between his shoulder blades. The door opened, and the gun slid outside, clattering across the boards and down to the murky ground below. Louis was helpless.

"You're a demon, Solène!" he screamed into the nothingness. "What did Vernand ever do to you?"

"He *was* such a good man, wasn't he? Strong, and handsome. I know why Nell kept him around." Louis wanted to retch. There was something vile in the way Solène talked about Vernand, like he was a warehouse district whore. "Shame I couldn't keep him around a bit longer," she purred. "I would've enjoyed that."

"Then why did you kill him?" Louis demanded.

Solène laughed. "As much as I would've liked to keep him for myself, he served his purpose. He brought me something I will enjoy *so much more.*" Louis' skin crawled as he felt a hand run up the back of his leg and stop at the small of his back giving the waistband of his pants a playful tug. He thrashed against the floor trying to break free of the force holding him down and Solène released him just long enough for Louis to turn over onto his back and scramble backwards away from her. Instantly, he realized he'd done exactly what she wanted. Unseen hands pushed him onto the planked floor. One hand rested heavily on his chest holding him down, while the other began playing with the curls in his hair. His hands clawed at air trying to pull her away but there was nothing to grab onto. Helpless, Louis flailed as Solène gently stroked his face and traced his lips with an invisible cold finger. Fear and revulsion surged through his body with every touch. Her laugh became a low sultry chuckle as he struggled against her.

"I won't give you what you want, Solène!"

A sharp crack of laughter. "You don't have to *give me* anything! I take what I want, cherie."

"Not everything, hag," Louis growled at her. "You can't take *Zéolie!*"

Solène roared in anger and slapped Louis hard across the face. There was a flash of blinding white light, then blackness.

Smells of burning wax and aged wood drifted through Louis' mind as he hovered on the edge of consciousness. Sounds of night creatures in the distance. Then, as he came closer to waking, pain. Aches all over his body. Willing his eyes open, he blinked against the brightness of the warm light. Candles burned in a ring around him. No longer was he on the hard wooden floor. Now, he lay in the same bed Zéolie had all those nights ago. Trying to bring the room into focus, he looked up and saw Vernand's hanging body was gone. Coming to grips with his surroundings, he saw all his clothes thrown in the corner across the room. Covering his bare skin was only a thin blanket. Memories of Solène's icy touch on his body flooded over him as he leaned over the side of the cot and vomited. A sultry low chuckle rumbled through the cabin as he slipped back into unconsciousness.

Searing pain brought him into a state of semi-consciousness, as though he'd been heavily sedated. Trying desperately to focus on what was happening around him, Louis blinked through the haze in his mind. He was still on the cot, but the blanket was gone. Symbols were slowly appearing along with the pain as an invisible knife carved into his skin. Even if they hadn't been blurred by whatever Solène gave him, he wouldn't have recognized them. Strange shapes with curls ending in hard angles. A circle with what looked like horns. Jagged lines and graceful curved moons. All of them angry and raw. Fresh warm blood oozed from the cuts, dripping down his chest and arms marring the figures as he slipped back into unconsciousness.

The next time he woke, there was an earthy fragrance filling the swamp cabin. He smelled it before at the house on Dauphine. Sage. Candles of different sizes and colors danced and flickered around him still. They burned but didn't drip. There was no wax running from them at all. Some seemed to hover just above him. He was sick and imagining things. None of this was possible. Blinking hard, he prayed for clarity, but everything remained blurred and ethereal.

A hand he could only feel moved up his chest. "Ah, cherie, you're awake," Solène cooed. "So strong, so young, so handsome." Her hands played along his bare chest and arms making their way to his legs, but he couldn't move to stop her. There was nothing to push away even if he could. His arms ached in places. The strange shapes she had carved into his body were red and crusted in dried blood cracking and flaking on his skin.

"What do you want, you wretch?" Louis demanded. His voice was raspy and dry.

"At the moment?" she asked sweetly. "*You.*"

"*Never!*" he tried to scream. It came out barely a whisper.

"Now, now, cherie, shhh." A cold finger settled on his mouth and he sank back into oblivion.

CHAPTER

FIFTEEN

S unlight played happily along the French Quarter rooftops casting long lazy shadows down the narrow streets. In the courtyard on Dauphine, high walls kept the heat of the afternoon sun at bay. Mama Nell and Zéolie were up to their elbows in dirt working in the herb garden when there came a pounding on the front door that echoed through the house. Neither of them moved to go open it since Vernand insisted that the women not open the door to possible danger. They went on with their work, but the pounding grew more insistent.

"Where's Vernand?" Zéolie asked straightening up and wiping sweat from her forehead with the back of her hand.

Mama Nell shook the dirt from her skirt. "I don't know. He'd gone back to the cabin for supplies an' take care of things there the other night, but I thought he'd be back by now." Since there was no one else to do it, Mama Nell went to the door.

"I'm comin'! You can stop your poundin'!" she called while Zéolie peeked through a side curtain to see who was there. It was a young man with an open cart. A large wooden crate and two other young men sat in the back. The dark young man at the door shifted uneasily as he stood on the front steps looking furtively over his shoulders at the other two. None of them seemed to want to be at the notorious house and the young one clearly drew the short straw to knock on the door.

"It's some men with a crate," Zéolie said over her shoulder. "A delivery maybe?"

Mama Nell nodded. "Could be. Vernand's had some things delivered here once before, but I'd'a thought he'd tell me to expect it." she said as she slid the bolt back. The priestess opened the door a bit and held it with her hip, keeping Zéolie largely shielded.

The young man on the stoop opened his mouth to speak but was taken aback by the exotic figure before him. His eyes wandered from her ankles all the way up to her mossy eyes. Whatever he had to say, he had completely forgotten.

"Can I help you, boy?" Mama Nell asked him, holding his gaze. Zéolie knew this wasn't the first time someone had been spellbound by her aunt and it probably wouldn't be the last.

The young man stuttered something about a delivery for Mademoiselle Cheval from Monsieur Vernand and waved the other two boys down from the cart to unload it.

It was heavy and awkward for the three of them to manage, but they finally got it inside. "Where do you want it, ma'am?" the first boy asked.

Mama Nell shrugged. "Well, since I don't know what's in it, I can't really say. Would'ya mind openin' it?"

The first boy sent another one out to the cart to fetch a pry bar. Wood creaked and cracked as they worked the edges of the lid away from the nails. Finally, it gave way and they lifted it off setting it to one side then wandered out to the cart to put the pry bar away and have a smoke before moving the crate where ever the priestess decided she wanted it. Under the lid was a layer of straw to protect the contents. Mama Nell grabbed a handful and pushed it aside. Her rich caramel face drained of color as she gripped the edges of the crate with white knuckles, swayed a moment, then fell in a heap on the floor. Zéolie shrieked and rushed to her aunt's side, skidding to her knees. Mama Nell was alive, but unconscious. Whatever was in that crate had shaken the priestess more than Zéolie thought was even possible. Slowly, Zéolie raised herself up from the floor and looked inside. There, curled in the straw, was Vernand with a frayed noose around his neck. Electricity rushed through her body and a thunderclap of rage and grief rattled the house as she screamed.

The three young men raced back into the house to see what happened. One rushed to Mama Nell's side and tried to revive her while the other two went to Zéolie. She stood trembling, staring into the wooden crate in the middle of the foyer floor. Following Zéolie's gaze, they saw the bloated ebony face in the straw and bolted from the house screaming for the police. Zéolie stood silhouetted in the open doorway like a statue.

Her mother's voice rang in her head, shrieking with her triumph. Fury and energy tangled inside Zéolie as she struggled to get control of her emotions. Cold fingers of sweat rolled between her shoulder blades and down her back as her blood boiled.

Officers who were stationed in the area came running to the house. As the first ones arrived to the gruesome scene, they sent an officer to go get more help. Two more officers were stationed outside the door to keep the gathering crowd at bay, while another saw to Zéolie and Mama Nell, who was slowly coming around but in shock.

"Please," Zéolie begged them. "I need to you to find Officer Saucier. *Please!*"

Two men darted in opposite directions to find Louis.

As much as she wanted to look away, Zéolie stood transfixed staring at the contorted face of the quiet man who protected her and loved her aunt. She couldn't bear the sight of him like that. "You didn't deserve this," she whispered. From the depths of her soul, an urge to do something began to rise to the surface. She didn't understand what it was but had learned enough from Mama Nell to follow her instincts. Closing her eyes, Zéolie held her hands out flat over the crate. A warm flood of energy flowed from the center of her chest up to her shoulders and down her arms. It wasn't a raging torrent like the energy of grief had been for her in the past. This was controlled and gentle as it coursed through her body and out the palms of her hands. After a few moments, the energy trickled to a stop and she opened her eyes. Vernand's face had completely changed. Gone was the bloated pained expression. In its place were his handsome features and a look of peaceful sleep. She knew the change was not for Vernand. It was to ease the pain for Mama Nell. And she had done it.

"Very good, cherie," Solène said. "I like him so much better that way. So handsome..."

Zéolie didn't like the tone in her mother's voice. It was sultry and despicable. "*You* did this to him. You *killed him*," she hissed.

"Yes," Solène admitted. "It's a shame, really. I enjoyed having him around for a tiny bit."

Zéolie felt sick to her stomach and her heart ached for Mama Nell. "*Why?* Why did you kill him? Why did you send him here like this?" Zéolie demanded.

Solène chuckled. "I sent him because I knew Nell would want her man back and I was finished with him." Her laugh was dark and cold. "And I killed him because he had served his purpose."

"What purpose?" Zéolie raged. "What have you *done?*" Solène dissolved into a fit of laughter. Whatever she had done, she was thoroughly pleased with herself.

One of the officers sent to fetch Louis returned and stood gasping for breath on the doorstep. "He's gone, mademoiselle. His door was left open, and I knocked, but there was no answer. I went inside but he was gone. So was his gun. Have you seen him today?"

Zéolie shook her head. "No, not today. He was going to come sometime after he took care of a few things, but we haven't seen him."

"I have men looking for him. We'll find him," the officer reassured her.

Solène shrieked with laughter and the walls vibrated with the sound. Glass rattled in the windows and the floorboards popped like gunfire. The officer clapped his hands over his ears to block the noise and whipped his head around looking for the owner of the voice. Zéolie dropped to her hands and knees in the foyer. Mama Nell stood in the doorway between the parlor and foyer clutching the door-frame. Both women felt the same sensation of dread and locked eyes with each other. In that instant, they knew.

"*Where is he, Solène? Where is Louis?*" Zéolie roared. Her slender white hands coiled into tight fists, fingernails digging into her palms. A tiny stream of blood began to pool in the creases of her clenched fingers. Tremors rocked her body as she fought to contain the energy of her anger. She had nowhere to direct the surging energy and was terrified she'd unleash something terrible on the innocent people surrounding her. "*Answer me, you witch!*"

Solène cackled. "What do you care? What's he to you?" her mother taunted.

She knew. The demon knew how Zéolie felt about Louis. "He's an officer of the law and has sworn to stop this madness. You can't terrorize this city forever!"

"Come now, cherie. 'An officer of the law'? Is that all?" Solène chuckled. "Well, since you don't want him, I'll keep him a while longer. I'm enjoying his company." Another sultry laugh. "*Immensely.*"

Zéolie threw her head back and screamed, her hands tearing at her black hair. She couldn't contain the energy and fury. Watching her niece losing control, Mama Nell lunged at her. "*No, Zéolie!*" she shrieked, but it was too late. As the priestess threw herself at Zéolie to stop the surge of energy, it flew from Zéolie's hands in a shower of white-hot sparks and struck her aunt in the chest. The priestess stumbled awkwardly back with her mossy eyes wide in shock. Convulsions wracked her frame in an obscene affront to her liquid grace. Her beautiful burgundy mouth contorted and foamed as she burned from the inside out. Slender fingers clawed at her throat that was closing fast as she made a desperate attempt to breathe.

Panic seized Zéolie yanking the breath from her chest. "What have I done?" she cried choked with sobs and shaking uncontrollably. Zéolie's hands burned so badly she was afraid to touch Mama Nell to help her. She held her hands in front of her, turning them over and staring at them. Small slender weapons. The foyer swirled and spun as she struggled to keep from fainting.

Two officers rushed to the suffering priestess and tried to save her as Zéolie watched dumbstruck and helpless. Not knowing what had caused the attack, the men had no idea what to do. Convulsions continued as they laid her on the floor trying to clear her airway. Their effort was noble but useless. White foam flecked with blood continued to bubble up from the priestess' insides. All Zéolie could do was watch with tears streaming down her pale cheeks as Mama Nell's precious life drained away. No herbs, no potions, no candles could help her now.

Throughout the house, Solène's triumphant laughing shook the very foundation sending spiderweb cracks shooting across the plaster and turning windowpanes to fractured lace. "Go to your dark lover, Nell!" she shrieked as the last gasping breath rattled from the priestess's body. "There's nothing left for you here, cherie. Nothing! *You are mine! Mine!*" Walls reverberated and shattered glass rained from the panes.

"*No!*" Zéolie screamed. She made a move for the front door but was stopped by an officer who grabbed her arm. "Let me go!" she ordered wrenching herself free of his grip. "I know where Louis is. She's taken him to the cabin."

"You aren't going after him, mademoiselle. It isn't safe," the officer pleaded with her.

Zéolie let out a crack of disgusted laughter. "Of course, it's not *safe!* Nothing is! As long as that madwoman is loose, *none of us are safe!*" She turned on her heel, her blazing black eyes face-to-face with the terrified officer, and hissed, "Did you see *nothing* that happened here? Do you think you can stop her with your little guns?"

The officer opened his mouth to say something but seemed to

think better of it. Dropping his eyes in defeat, he pleaded, "At least let someone go with you."

"Don't you understand? She'll *kill you all*. No. I go alone. It's me she wants. This madness has to stop. It ends now, and it ends with me." Zéolie tore open the front door and marched down the front steps, her dark hair flying loose in the gathering wind. "A carriage. *Now!*" she ordered one of the officers standing in the street. He whistled down a passing driver and helped her inside.

The young officer who tried to stop her stood in the doorway with a look of terror and pleading in his eyes. "Please, mademoiselle. Be careful."

With a determined nod, she closed the door and the carriage tore through the streets of the Quarter towards the north swamps. With any luck, there was something in the cabin she could use. Something, anything that could help her face down the demon. But most importantly, Louis was there. Panic ruthlessly seized her stomach as doubt wracked her mind. How the hell was she supposed to stop a witch that strong by herself and with power she could barely control?

METAL-RIMMED CARRIAGE WHEELS rattled over the cobbled streets of the Quarter as it raced north. Inside, the heat and fear grew oppressive and made her nauseous, so she pulled the curtain aside to let some air move through. It whipped her hair across her face but didn't help cool the heat that seemed to be radiating from inside her as much as the humid air outside. Stench of waste in the alleys clinging in the thick air made her stomach roll.

Soon the buildings parted, and the air changed. It was as heavy and humid as the Quarter, but at least the foulness was gone. Shouts and carriage rattling gave way to quiet as she left the city and neared the swamps surrounding it to the north. Only the singsong of her mother broke the relative peace. There was no mocking of Zéolie's doubt and fear, which meant Solène was preoccupied with Louis. The swamp was wild and dangerous, but nothing compared to the demon lurking at its core. The view from the carriage window was deceptively serene as she looked out at the lazy egrets and cranes standing among the tall marsh grass. Once in a while, one would spread its huge wings and slowly lift off with deep pumps of graceful wings to fly across the watery land. The birds looked so content out there. So oblivious to the evil around them. As the landscape changed from flat grassy marsh to thick cypress stands, the carriage rattled to a stop bringing her out of her thoughts and back to the reality of her grisly errand.

The driver reluctantly set Zéolie down at the edge of the swamp. The same place she and Angelie started their fateful journey. Even in the fading afternoon light, the swamp seemed shrouded in darkness from within. Cypress trees rose high against the layers of clouds that seemed to be sinking towards her. Black lace of Spanish moss swayed and whipped in the gathering wind. Standing at the edge of the water that had been inky black the night Zéolie first made this trip, she noticed the daylight didn't change it much. The dark water weaving through higher patches of ground was still, save for the few ripples stirred by the wind. Grasses swayed ahead of her letting her know where the ground was more or less solid enough to walk on. *Even the grasses lie*, she thought. *Nothing is solid here.*

As the storm gathered overhead, memories of the last harrowing night in the swamp swirled with the wind and washed over her. Zéolie hands stung more with each tentative step into the tangled depths as electricity swirled around her, amplified by the building clouds above. Broken reeds and crushed grass marked the almost invisible path to the heart of the swamp. Intensely aware of the sounds around her and every movement in the marsh, she walked steadily on. The journey was long and perilous, but nothing in the swamp could frighten her now. Zéolie had seen more terror and evil in the Crescent City than the swamp itself could throw at her. Determination pushed her feet forward and love drove every beat of her heart. Only her mother's content singing and laughter sent a shiver through her as she tried not to think about what was putting the witch in such a pleasant mood.

Exhausted and filthy, she finally came to the open space where Mama Nell's cabin stood. Thunder rumbled in the distance signaling the storm's imminence, but she didn't care. Static electricity built around her and Zéolie's hands tingled with the strength of the gathering energy. Stopping at a clump of cattail reeds on the outskirt of the clearing, she rested a moment resisting the urge to rush headlong towards the cabin and Louis. If she was going to make any kind of stand against Solène, she needed all her strength and her wits about her.

Reeds swayed in the wind that whistled a low mournful cry. Her mother's song took on a hollowness that made her voice mysterious and otherworldly. Solène sang a slow verse that Zéolie couldn't understand but was full of richness and beauty. Minor notes seemed to harmonize with the sounds of the wind itself. Ethereal, ancient, and mystical. Music seemed to be coming from everything around her in a rich chorus. Swirling, rising, falling. It was hypnotic.

Trying to regain control, her mind raced through everything that happened in the past weeks. So many people died trying to protect her. So much fear and madness. Murders and pain that she was powerless to stop. As her own weakness settled heavily on her shoulders, Zéolie sank to her knees. What could she possibly do against a force like her mother? One that was ever-present but never there. Solène could control life and death with a word, a thought. What could Zéolie do against that? She had no control over whatever the strange powers were that she inherited, and no one left to guide her. She was alone and a loose cannon. Could she risk using the powers she possessed? She was responsible for the death of her aunt and had nearly killed herself trying to save the nun who died helping her. Zéolie stopped short of thinking about what could happen if the energy misfired and struck Louis. She wasn't ready for this and her mother was counting on it.

Between the swaying reeds, she could see the dark silhouette of Nell's cabin. A shadow passed in front of one of the windows. It was fleeting, and she couldn't make out what it was, but it was definitely there. Zéolie's rising heartbeat thundered in her ears with the storm as she watched the house. What was she going to do? She had no plan at all, only instinct to guide her. Getting to Louis was all that mattered.

Zéolie crept closer to the cabin with the wind clawing at her skirt, winding the fabric around her legs making it difficult to walk. Still she pressed slowly on, straining her ears for any sound that could tell her what was happening inside. Solène's mystical song had gone quiet. Her mother was distracted by something and Zéolie hoped it was enough to give her the advantage. Easing her way up the staircase, she prayed the steps wouldn't creak and give her presence away. The warped front door was shut, and a curtain drawn in front of the window next to it concealing her approach as well as anything inside. She put her ear to the door but heard nothing. Standing in the swamp she had been sure she saw a shadow inside the house. Someone must be inside, but there was no way to know where they were and what was happening.

With measured movements, she put a stinging hand flat on the damp wooden door. Lichen coating the warped wood in the dampness of the swamp was soft and slick on her fingers. Her other hand found the handle and pushed gently, but the door didn't budge. She leaned more of her weight against it. Nothing. It was locked. Frustrated, she placed both palms on the door and rested her forehead on the backs of her hands. *This door can't be locked. I have to get inside. Please!* Zéolie's palms tingled, and a whisper hissed from the edges of the door. Zéolie started and took a step back, then tentatively placed her hand on the door again. It moved silently on its hinges, opening slightly. A thread of faint golden light shot across the damp covered porch. Standing frozen on the threshold, she waited to be discovered, but there was no sign of movement from the interior of the cabin. Letting her breath out slowly, trembling hands pushed the door open another inch.

Through the opening, Zéolie saw the familiar room she sat in before listening to Mama Nell shake the foundations of everything she knew of her family history. Shelves of dusty old books, baskets and bunches of dried herbs hanging from the ceiling, and old tired furniture. The curtains were drawn except for the one Zéolie had seen the shadow through from the reeds. Light flickered from somewhere across the room leaving most of the cabin in darkness. Quieting her own rapid breathing, she heard a faint moan from deep in the recesses within.

Louis. He was alive! A shiver of relief ran through her. She eased the door open another few inches, her foot hovering just above the threshold. Mingled with her panic to get to Louis was a sickening feeling about what she was really doing. Zéolie tried to focus on rescuing the man she loved but standing on the threshold brought the full magnitude of what she had done crashing down on her. Zéolie came to Solène on her own. Unforced. The witch didn't want to hurt her. Zéolie knew that and finally understood why. Her mother wanted the power she possessed, and the demon would stop at nothing until she controlled the daughter who inherited it. All Zéolie could hope for now was another way out. Some way to take her mother down without becoming a monster herself. *I've come willingly. If I step through this door, I've come to her on my own. She's won.* In that moment, Zéolie didn't care. She would deal with Solène, but first she had to get to Louis.

On the far side of the room, surrounded by candles, was the same bed where she spent nights of troubled oblivion being tended by her aunt. Louis had been there, too. She knew that now. Another low moan came from the direction of the bed. "Louis!" she whispered. Zéolie scanned the room looking for any sign of her mother, who had gone eerily silent. Nothing.

Cautiously, Zéolie made her way to the bed and Louis. He was unconscious and barely recognizable. Bruises covered his face and neck. On his cheekbone under one eye was an angry cut that had a dried stream of blood below it. The other eye was black and nearly swollen shut. Dark sandy curls were plastered to his forehead by sweat and his breathing was rapid and shallow. Zéolie choked back a sob as she looked down at him realizing Solène had beaten him within an inch of his life. Kneeling by the bed, she pulled back the pile of bedclothes to cool him. It was only then she realized he was bound to the bed. Sigils had been carved up both of his arms and scabbed over. Like the candles in Zéolie's parlor, her mother had marked him with her intentions. Strips of ripped cloth were tied tightly around his wrists and the tarnished brass rungs of the headboard. Zéolie clawed at the knots desperately, but each time she worked one loose, it would constrict tighter than before slithering around his hands like vines.

Frantically she searched for something to cut the bindings. On Mama Nell's work bench next to a large white candle, was the same small silver dagger with intricate symbols carved into it that she'd used to carve the candles in her parlor. On the tip of the blade was a dark dried line of Louis' blood. Her mother used the same knife to carve the sigils into Louis' skin. Before Zéolie could touch it, a spark leaped from the dagger to her finger and shocked her. *Damn that storm*, she thought jerking back her hand. Static electricity in the air was dangerously high making her skin tingle. She had no choice but to touch the knife and cut Louis free. Grabbing the dagger, Zéolie felt a surge of electricity shoot painfully up her arm, but she gripped the handle tight. Racing back to the bedside, she knelt and began mercilessly sawing at the fabric bindings. Nothing was happening. *Why would Mama Nell keep a dull knife?* thought Zéolie. She tested the blade by lightly running it over the palm of her hand. Effortlessly, a long thin cut opened, dripping fresh blood onto the wooden planks of the floor. It wasn't the knife. Clutching the dagger, she tried to push the growing panic from her mind. She was rapidly losing control of her emotions and needed to rein them back in before they consumed her. Closing her eyes, she saw roots shooting through the floorboards down into the swamp below the house. They reached deep, holding her steady and calm as she grounded herself. Zéolie breathed in deeply and felt the air fill her lungs then pass back through her lips with the exhale. A warm silvery light settled around her. Camille.

With steady hands, Zéolie held the knife above the bindings and slowly lowered it. As the blade touched the fabric, it began to burn through. A tendril of smoke curled up from the blade. Letting the weight of the blade do the work, she watched as it slid through the cloth freeing Louis' hands.

He let out a small groan as his arms fell limp above his head. Zéolie climbed up on the bed and pulled both of his ice-cold hands to his chest. Frantically, she began rubbing them trying to get his circulation flowing again, but the blood from her own cut hand smeared his hands in sticky crimson. Ripping an edge of the sheet, she bound her own hand and kept rubbing life back into his. Louis stirred in the bed as the warmth returned to his tingling hands. Dark blue eyes fluttered open, at least as far as the swollen one could. "Zéolie," he whispered through cracked dry lips.

Sobs and laughter mixed as relief flooded over her. "Shh. Don't try to talk yet. We have to get you out of here."

Louis shook his head. "No, go. Solène can't find you here. She—she's a *demon*, Zéolie. She's done—" he choked as tears ran unchecked from his swollen bloody eyes. "She's done terrible things. I won't let you risk yourself for me."

"I'm not leaving you for her to torture! We're getting out of here."

"Zéolie, she killed Vernand."

Zéolie's eyes fell and a shiver of cold and guilt ran through her. "I know," she replied in a strained whisper. "She sent his body to Mama Nell in a crate. I—I lost control. I was so angry and hurt. I-—she tried to stop me, but she just got in the way. I—*I killed her.*" Great heaving sobs wracked her body as the weight of what she had done broke over her in a tidal wave of pain. "So many have died because of me. So many..."

Louis pulled himself up on his elbows and held her as she cried kneeling on the floor beside him. Scabs cracked and oozed as his arms tightened around the woman he desperately loved. He had no words. Nothing he could say could take away the horror her life had become. All Louis could do was hold her. Soon, the sobbing subsided as she gathered her wits about her once again. "Zéolie," he said gently, "she can't find you here."

Nodding and wiping tears with the blood-soaked bandage on her hand, she asked, "Do you know where she is? I can't hear her." Louis shook his head slowly. "Gone or not, she's not interfering," Zéolie said. "We have to try to get out of this place while we can."

Zéolie stood watch at the door as Louis pulled himself to his feet and found his clothes. Once he was dressed, he sat back on the bed to catch his breath. Solène's wrath at his resistance to her advances had been brutal and took its toll on his strength. Once he had his wind back, he joined Zéolie at the door. She was still clutching the dagger. Louis wasn't sure what good that would be against the swamp witch, but since he had no gun, it would have to do.

"Have you seen her?" she asked, inching her way across the porch.

He shook his head. "No, I've just heard her. And... felt her." His stomach lurched as he forced the bile burning his throat back down.

"Let's hope we don't see her," Zéolie said as they made their way tentatively down the warped front steps to the soggy ground below.

Solène's laughter roared over their heads. "Darling, girl! Would that really be so bad?"

Zéolie and Louis froze in their tracks searching for the source of the voice. She had to be there somewhere. She had to be flesh and blood this time. The voice was different. It was solid, yet thinner. No echoing richness this time. "There!" Louis hissed at Zéolie, pointing above their heads to the roof where a shadowed form danced in the wind.

Lightning flashed and Zéolie saw the same wild-haired crazed-eyed face she saw in the window the night her father was killed. "*Solène!*"

"Now, now, cherie. Where are you off to in such a hurry?" she mocked from her perch on the roof. With a wave of her hand, a wall of flames sprang up around the clearing in the swamp. Strange swaying sentinels seemed to emerge in the eerie light where the quiet cypress trees had stood an instant before. Above the flames, gaps in the approaching black storm clouds were painted in deep reds, oranges, and purples with the setting sun. If it hadn't been paired with the fiery scene around them, it would have been beautiful. Against the black shadows of the swamp and the maniacal laughter of Solène, it was terrifying. Hell in the sky.

As they watched, Solène danced and sang triumphantly, spinning and twirling precariously on the steep pitched roof. She had them trapped and was enjoying the moment of victory immensely. "Don't go, *cherie*. Stay with me and Louis!" she cackled. "Twenty-one years I've lived for this! You came on your *own*, Zéolie! I *knew* you would! I knew you couldn't resist coming for Louis. I can't blame you, cherie." Solène dove onto her stomach and slid down the pitch to the edge of the roof, clutching the edge and peering down at her prizes. "He's *irresistible*." She licked her red lips and beckoned him with the curl of her finger.

Louis lunged toward Solène and roared at her, "*Goddamn you! You had to take what you would not be given! You demon witch!*" he snarled. Zéolie stood horrified as the meaning of it all sank in. Rage and nausea threatened to burst from her body as she fought to control it.

Solène sprang to her feet on the roof, impossibly nimble on the steep pitch, and thrust the palm of her hand out towards Louis. He flailed backwards like a rag doll as the witch threw her head back and laughed, pulling in the energy from the growing storm. Silvery sparks danced along the edges of her swirling black dress as the static electricity moved through her. "Come, Zéolie! Come to me! You are *mine*."

Zéolie ran over to where Louis lay in a heap on the wet ground. Lightning flashed, and thunder rolled around them. The flame fence swirled and lapped dangerously close. It seemed to be closing tighter without consuming any of the landscape. Desperately, she pulled Louis to his feet and held on to him.

Reassured that Louis wasn't hurt, Zéolie turned her attention back to Solène. She had no idea how to fight her mother in the flesh and had only defeated her in mental battles with the help of Camille. Nothing in Mama Nell's lessons prepared her for the terror in front of them. Zéolie may just as well have been fighting blind.

All around her, electricity from the storm buzzed on her skin. Zéolie harnessed a storm before and almost killed herself in the process, but she had to try something. Anything. Solène danced on the rooftop of the cabin laughing and singing. Her mother was so certain of her triumph that she was oblivious to Zéolie's thoughts. As the energy gathered in her hands, Zéolie's palms tingled and grew warm. Fingers of her left hand closed tightly around the knife at her side as she raised her right palm level with her shoulder, then thrust the energy at her mother as hard as she could.

Solène had seen the movement and braced for the impact. The witch planted her feet and opened her arms wide. As the surge of energy met her open arms, Solène seemed to drink it in. Her red lips split into a devilish grin and her eyes rolled back into her head in ecstasy from the power she was absorbing. Zéolie was drained, but her mother was stronger.

Zéolie knew she couldn't keep throwing energy at Solène but wasn't sure what to do next.

"What's happening?" Louis called to her over the popping flames and rumbling thunder.

"She's pulling the energy from me. My power only adds to hers!" she shouted. The sounds around them were deafening. The fire, storm, and the maniacal laughter of her mother drowned out their voices.

"Can you use something out here to take her down so it's not your energy directly?" he asked.

Solène cackled from the roof. "She can't hurt me, Louis. Poor *delicious* fool that you are!" Solène reached out and he could once more feel her vile unseen hands on his body. Revulsion surged through him, but he didn't fight her. If he could hold the witch's attention, it might buy Zéolie some time.

While Solène was entertaining herself with Louis, Zéolie worked as fast as she could to focus the energy she was building before Solène could stop her. Breaking the connection to the electricity of the storm was the only hope Zéolie had. But, how? Solène was stronger than the two of them, but she wouldn't come down from the roof of the cabin, even to get her hands on Louis. There was something about that position that held some power.

Panicked and determined, Zéolie looked for anything she could use to bring her mother down. Her own rage and frustration began to surge threatening her control. "There's nothing here but *trees!*" As the words escaped her lips, a cypress to her right began to sway wildly. The fire in the branches changed from reds and oranges to white-hot. "No, not white-hot!" Zéolie gasped. "*It's silver! Camille!*"

Zéolie jammed the dagger into the waistband of her skirt and focused all the strength she had on the tree adding her power to her grandmother's. Camille was breaking Solène's grip on the cypress so Zéolie could use it. Closing her eyes to block the distraction of the inferno around her and her mother's sultry advances on Louis, she began to visualize the deep roots releasing the earth as the cypress stretched its knees. Slowly, she brought her hands up and the tree groaned and cracked as it rose out of the spongy ground. With a swift jerk of her arms towards the cabin, Zéolie sent the flaming cypress hurtling toward her mother. The tree hit its target and sent Solène toppling backwards in a shower of silver sparks.

Breaking free of Solène's grip, Louis sank to the ground

exhausted from resisting her. Zéolie rushed to his side, but he waved her away. "I'm fine. Finish her."

Zéolie nodded and looked up at the roof. "I can't see her!"

A low rumbling laugh surrounded Zéolie and Solène's hand appeared at the top of the roof. Gripping the peak, she began to claw her way back into her position of power. "*Foolish girl!*" she roared.

Feet planted, arms down at her sides, and palms out, Zéolie grounded herself at the base of the cabin stilts and focused on her grandmother. She needed Camille's help to destroy the demon dancing on the rooftop above her. "Camille," she whispered. "I need you! You know what she is. You have to help me stop her!"

Solène glared down at Zéolie and snarled with rage. Her mother held a hand flat out over the swamp water. The blackness began to boil and heave. With a loud sucking sound, a boat broke through the inky surface, dripping murky water and slime, and hurtled towards her. Zéolie dove to the ground and the boat crashed into the flaming ring of trees, steam from the wet hull hissing in the heat. Zéolie's summoning Camille to the fight only fueled the witch's fury and madness. Solène held her hands out towards her daughter, and Zéolie could feel the energy being pulled from her body. *How is she doing this?* she thought, panicking as she grew weaker. "Camille!" she screamed into the empty spaces around her. "*Where are you?*"

Solène roared with laughter but kept her hold on Zéolie.

Zéolie reached for the rosary that had been tucked into her shirt. It was gone. Her eyes and hands searched the ground around her, but in vain. At the edge of the ring of trees, she finally saw the crucifix glint in the firelight. Zéolie scrambled toward the rosary as sparks rained down on it. Wooden beads burned and the crucifix glowed red. Desperate, she grabbed it anyway, screaming as the crucifix branded the palm of her hand.

"Sorry, mon cherie," Solène cooed from the roof. "You've lost your tie to her. Camille can't help you now!"

The swamp seemed to swim and swirl around Zéolie as Solène

drained her power. Weak knees threatened to betray her as she pulled the dagger out and held it tight. It was all she had now.

"You are *mine*, child," her mother thundered overhead. "You always have been. *The power we will have together will be unstoppable!* You can have anything you want in the world. Anything!"

The dagger in Zéolie's hand began to grow warm. In that moment, she knew what she had to do. There was no other way to stop the nightmare.

Seething, Zéolie yelled over the storm. "*I want my father back, Solène!* Can you give me that?"

Her mother raged. "Why would you want *that*? Julien was so weak, and you are so strong, child! He wasn't worthy of either of us! He was a *fool*," she spat.

"And Angelie?" Zéolie screamed. "And Vernand, and Mama Nell!" Solène shrieked as Zéolie listed the victims of her mother's nightmarish reign of terror. "And Father Antoine!" Solène's hands tore at her hair that was standing on end in the electrical storm around her, wild and black. Zéolie was pushing her mother to the brink of rage and madness and she knew it. "Did you think I would love you after all you've done? No one can love a *monster*!" Solène contorted in her demonic wrath. "I will *never* be yours, Solène! *Never!*" Zéolie raised the dagger high in the air making sure her mother could see what she was doing. "I'll *die* first!"

"Zéolie!" Louis screamed. "*No!*"

Lightning flashed in rapid-fire as the storm closed in making the swamp pulse with movement around her. As Zéolie brought the dagger down hard toward her chest, Solène reacted. Zéolie's arms yanked backwards and pinned themselves behind her, wrists crossed at her lower back. Screaming, she lurched her shoulders in a vain struggle to free her hands to finish what she started.

Louis looked on in horror at what she had tried to do and her struggle against her mother. Still weak, he crawled over to Zéolie who was fighting furiously against the invisible bonds to free her hands and the dagger. "Don't do this. *Please!*" he cried. "There has to be another way!"

Zéolie shook her head with her black eyes wide and wild. "There is *no other way.*"

"This is madness, Zéolie!" Louis cried as terror seized him. "I won't let you do this! I won't let that demon hurt you!"

"Louis, listen to me!" Zéolie cried over the raging storm and flames. "Solène doesn't want to *hurt me*. She wants to *control me*." Her voice dropped as she looked into his eyes. "You have to let me do this. I came on my own." Tears were filling her eyes as she spoke. "She's won if I don't do this! Don't let her turn me into that!"

Flames licked the rooftop of the cabin behind Zéolie and the wind lifted her hair. For an instant in the fiery eeriness of the swamp, the innocence and beauty in front of him contorted into the madwoman shrieking on the roof. Then, in a sickening moment of clarity, he understood what Zéolie was doing and why. It was the only way to end the rampage and he knew it. So did she. Solène would hunt her relentlessly until she had what she wanted. So much pain, so much destruction, so much death. In a trance of grief and exhaustion, he took Zéolie by her shoulders to stop her struggling. He looked deep into her eyes and nodded.

Zéolie stopped panicking and looked up at Louis and the heart-break in his eyes. She did her best to create a shield around her thoughts and words before she spoke. Solène couldn't know what they were saying. "Louis, you know what you have to do. She won't stop killing until she has what she wants." Tears streaked down her mud-splattered face as she spoke. "She wants *me*, Louis, and I can't let her. The two of us together are too much power to control with madness. I can't stop her! I'm not strong enough. *She'll kill them all to get to me.*" She choked on her words. "Madame Marchon, Celeste, Lisestte, Mother Micheaux. *All of them!*" Her black eyes pleaded with him. "She'll kill *you* when you don't amuse her anymore. *I can't let that happen! You know what you have to do!*" she hissed. "*Please, Louis,*" Zéolie begged. "*Please,* don't let me become that. *Please save me!*"

Louis nodded slowly. He knew. He had known since Solène brought him to the cabin. She wouldn't stop until she had control of the power of her daughter, and as long as Zéolie resisted, no one in New Orleans was safe from her wrath. But if Zéolie went to her to save the ones she loved, the amount of power Solène would possess would make her a formidable force and he couldn't allow that, either. This was bigger than the two of them. He had no choice. It had to end.

Louis wrapped his arms around Zéolie. His left arm slid up her back and grabbed her hair at the nape of her neck to hold her close and still. She was strong but trembling. His right hand took the dagger from hers still pinned behind her. Louis' lips came down hard on Zéolie's. His tears melted into hers as he brought the knife up to her chest. He had to find the right place so she wouldn't suffer. It had to be quick. Pulling her closer and never releasing her kiss, he pushed the dagger between Zéolie's ribs and into her heart.

Zéolie's breath caught in her throat as the warmth of the blade penetrated her skin. A surge of electricity coursed through her as the life began to drain away. Louis finally released his grip on her and the dagger, hands hanging limply at his sides. She stumbled back a step and looked into his grieving face. Louis watched transfixed with horror as blood poured from her chest and her beautiful face drained white. She nodded at him and smiled. "I love you, Louis." she whispered. "I am my own, now. Je suis mon propre."

"I love you, Zéolie," he said, his voice tight and strained. "With all that I am. I love you. Vous êtes votre propre, et je suis à vous."

Lightning glittered on the silver hilt of the dagger in her chest as Zéolie sank lifelessly to the ground. Her mental shield against Solène died with her and the witch's wrath burst forth throwing Louis to the ground. "*Fool!*" she shrieked. "*What have you done?*" Solène raised her hands to the sky to harness the energy she needed to destroy the man who had taken from her only thing she had lived for. In her fury, she lost control and pulled everything she could from the raging storm. It was too much, even for Solène. Deafening thunder exploded overhead, and a bolt of lightning shot straight down to her hands and poured electricity into her. The house smoldered beneath her feet as her body ignited. Louis watched in a bizarre mixture of revulsion and relief as Solène's hair burst into a flaming mane around her. He couldn't look away as her skin bubbled and peeled away from the bone. Roaring and popping, flames licked at her dress as the wind whipped it into wild swirls around her. Black smoke belched forth from the gaping hole in the roof that she balanced perilously on the edge of, screaming in rage and pain. Sparks flew like fireworks against the darkness.

Numbly, Louis watched the witch writhe in agony on the roof. He was empty. A shell of a man standing lost in the swamp. Nothing was real anymore. This wasn't happening. There wasn't a witch burning alive on the roof of a dead Voodoo priestess' cabin in the deep black heart of the swamp. The love of his life wasn't lying at his feet dead by his own hands. Firelight rippled on the hilt of the dagger in Zéolie's heart. There was nothing left for him here. Nothing.

Louis knelt beside Zéolie's body and kissed her lips, already cold. She was gone. She loved him, and she was gone. It was his hand that drove the knife into her heart. Louis reached out to the handle of the dagger shining silver in the lightning. It was warm, but Zéolie was cold. His trembling hands curled around it and he slowly drew the knife out of its resting place. No blood spurted out. Her heart wasn't pushing it through her body anymore.

Her heart. Her blood. Her blood was on the blade. Louis ran a finger through the crimson that dripped from the point of the knife. Her life. Her blood. Her heart.

Louis watched as Solène's incinerated body tumbled down from the top of the cabin inferno. He bent and kissed Zéolie's icy lips one last time then raised the dagger high, looking at the beauty of the blade. The handle was engraved with intricate carvings and words he had come to know. Tu appartiens à toi-même.

"And I am yours," he said as he brought the blade down hard into his ribs, sinking it into his heart.

EPILOGUE

Mother Micheaux stood alone in front of the open crypts in the wall of the cemetery. Before her, small candles burned on the two slabs illuminating the cold stone in a rich warm glow. She didn't notice. There was nothing else in the world but the two polished wood coffins before her.

Side by side, they were set in the openings in the wall. Side by side they rested. Side by side they died for something bigger than they were. Side by side forever.

Trembling white hands rested on each as she prayed. There were no rehearsed prayers for things like this. No words of the Mass addressed it. No requiem would be appropriate. The words were her own and they would be shared with no one but her God.

When she was finished, her aged fingers ran the length of the flowers set upon the shining coffins. On each, a single black rose.

"C'est fini."

With a nod to the grave masons, she watched them seal the tombs. Brick by agonizing brick, the coffins slowly disappeared from view. Except for two strings. Strings that were tied to the wrists of each who rested there inside the darkness of the boxes. Her mind drifted to those who hung bells from strings in hopes that their loved ones lost to yellow fever were somehow still alive, praying they would hear a bell ring from the grave signaling life inside. Foolishness, she knew, to hang bells here for the two who lost their lives this way. As hopeless as it seemed, she tied two small brass bells to the strings. They tinkled softly as she let them go. Silently she prayed the sound would be heard again. Bowing slightly to the man who would take the watch for the night, she turned to go. Her footsteps on the stones sounded hollow and empty as she walked through the iron gate that shut behind her with a clang. When the last of the metallic echo rang softly and faded, in the gloom of the cemetery wall, two candles began to flicker and pop as two black roses slowly turned red.

ACKNOWLEDGMENTS

There are so many people who, in one way or another, were responsible for helping this book go from my head to your hand. Many heartfelt thanks to the following in no particular order.

My parents who encouraged me to read everything and to find my own creative voice. Who knew all those nights reading Shel Silverstein to tiny me and taking slightly bigger me to the library for another Georgette Heyer book would lead to this?

My daughter Gracie who said she didn't want to read the manuscript because she was waiting until she could hold the finished book in her hands. Thank you for being my cheerleader and never being embarrassed of your odd bohemian mom.

My son Cam who did actually read the manuscript. Thank you for reading the early stuff and not picking apart my mistakes!

My youngest daughter Luna who makes one hell of a guerrilla marketer by telling everyone, and I mean everyone, about my book.

My mom who not only reads the books once they're finished but hashes out plots with me before words ever make it to the page. Thank you for every last thing you've done to support me, creatively and as your daughter. There are a lot of good moms out there, but I've got the best!

My daddy who always asked how things were going with my book and listened patiently as I babbled. I miss you so much.

My brother Adam, sister-in-law Daravanh, and my nephews Isaac and Eli, to whom I am their Auntie Penguin, for being great cheerleaders and voices of sanity when I lose my own.

Margaret Hall, who is more family than friend and has the best all caps celebratory texts ever.

CRESCENT CITY SIN, BOOK 2 IN THE CRESCENT CITY SERIES

In the Crescent City, darkness blurs the lines between sinners and saints.Having been brought back through the veil after her death, Zéolie wakes to find she's being cared for by the mother superior. Secrets are slowly revealed as Mother Micheaux explains her connection to the past Zéolie's father kept hidden all her life. Once her strength has returned, Zéolie tries to ease back into her home and life without Louis, but soon finds herself helping a young man who mistakenly shows up at her house looking for his long-lost mother. Feeling compassion for the young man who is far from his home in France, she and the Marchon girls attempt to help him locate his mother while making him feel welcome.

Julien, the young man, finds himself strangely drawn to Zéolie and slowly loses his heart to her, but his feelings aren't returned when Zéolie makes a new discovery that changes her life once more. Jilted, Julien unleashes his grief in the form of magical power he didn't know he had and finds comfort in the friendship of a local madame. Out of control and angry, he succumbs to the darkness inside of him and the taunting voice of a raging spirit hungry for revenge.

Can Zéolie and her magical menagerie pull Julien back from the edge of hell, or will the past take them all down? Walk down the gritty dark streets of 1830s New Orleans where the line between sinner and saint is as blurred as the line between life and death.

About the Author

Originally from south Louisiana, Nola Nash now makes her home in Brentwood,Tennessee, and spends most of her time in Franklin. Growing up in Baton Rouge, she spent long hours onstage or backstage in the local community theaters. Her biggest writing inspiration was the city of New Orleans that gave her at an early age a love of the magic, mystery, and history.

When she isn't writing, Nola is an online high school instructional coach or interviewing authors on Dead Folks Tales and BYOB on Authors on the Air Global Radio Network. She also considers tacos and coffee major food groups.

ALSO BY NOLA NASH

Made in the USA
Middletown, DE
02 May 2023